Hostage

Hostage

HERBERT HARKER

BOOKCRAFT
Salt Lake City, Utah

*To missionaries everywhere this book
is affectionately dedicated, and
especially to five who held nothing back
in devotion to their calling—
Val, John, Lori, Brian, and Sally*

Library of Congress Catalog Card Number: 88-71565

ISBN 0-88494-671-1

First Printing, 1988

Printed in the United States of America

All characters in this book
are fictitious, and any resemblance
to actual persons, living or dead,
is purely coincidental.

One

If you ever get lost driving in the Rocky Mountain foothills somewhere east of the Great Divide, you might stop in a town to ask your way, and find that it is called Sweet Willow. Chances are you'll be at the barbershop, it being on the first corner as you enter the business block. And my dad, who cuts the town's hair, will say to you something like, "Mister, I can see that you are a man of the world. How is it that, after all your perambulations, you can arrive at the center of the universe and innocently ask, 'Where am I?' This, sir, is the town of Sweet Willow—home of the clearest sky, the freshest breeze . . . Do you realize, sir, that in this town it has sometimes been necessary to arrest an otherwise faultless citizen for imbibing too much intoxicating air? This is the true Elysium, sir—the same as that one celebrated by the ancients in story and song."

By this time, of course, you are convinced that you have wandered into a certifiable asylum, and you can hardly wait to get back to your car and down the road. But before that can happen my dad will laugh and offer you a cup of hot Postum if the day is cold, or lemonade if it's hot, and while you talk Dad will go on cutting hair, and like as not you'll end up getting a haircut, too. So when it happens to you, remember you're not the first. Over the years we've had all kinds. One portly, perfumed woman rolled down her electric window and sniffed, "How quaint!"

I wouldn't call Sweet Willow quaint, though in this high tech world it is a little old-fashioned. We still have bazaars and barbecues and ball games—the three B's, that is. The horse race is something else. The Sweet Willow Derby, or Straddle, as it is affectionately called, is the social event of the year. Everybody goes, and half of those who go, it seems, enter a horse in the great race. For most of them, the thought of winning is a forlorn hope. For the past several years, the competition has been strictly between the Fenders and the Rhals.

I had ridden in horse races since I was knee-high to a grasshopper, but last year was the first time I had ever been out there in the middle of the Sweet Willow Straddle, elbow to elbow with the other riders, and I wouldn't have traded my place for a trip to Disneyland. I didn't have a prayer of winning, but I was there, my blood going as fast as the pounding of the horses' hooves as we turned into the stretch. My eyes were blurred by the wind and dust, my mind terrified and exultant all together, and my ears filling with the shouts of the crowd as we rushed toward the line. I could make out Ry Fender and Fetch Rhal out in front, but I couldn't tell who was ahead. Then it was over; I felt that last wild lifting rush that comes when you cross the line, and then the slow unravelling and turning back toward the judges' stand to get the results. I wished I'd quit growing, so I could spend the rest of my life in a racing saddle.

Out behind the grandstand we walked our horses to cool them off. I found Ry Fender walking beside me. I said, "Tough luck, Ry."

"We beat them last year," he said.

"That new mare of theirs runs like a cheetah," I said. I had read not long before that the cheetah is the fastest animal on four legs. I looked across at Ry. He was about five years older than me, and since he never came into the barbershop, we hadn't gotten to know each other very well. I think his mother cut his hair.

"I hate to lose," he said.

"It was close," I told him. "I heard them saying how close it was."

"Close!" He said it like it was a dirty word. "I'd rather be last than second place."

Well, I doubted that. I had been last a couple of times in my brief riding career; I knew what it felt like.

Ry was not very tall, but he was husky. He had curly dark hair, and a smile like a sunny day. But he wasn't smiling now. "I'm just too heavy," he said. "It's not fair to Fiddler, asking him to carry a tub like me, and win too."

Actually, Ry was no tub. He looked like he was solid bone and muscle, but what he said was true. He had grown too big for a jockey.

"There's something I want to talk to you about," he said. "I wasn't going to mention it yet, but . . . No big secret, you understand."

"I won't say anything, if that's what you mean," I said. I couldn't imagine what he was talking about. "Nobody will find out from me, I promise."

Ry couldn't hold still a minute. Even walking up and down with Fiddler, he seemed to keep twitching, or jiving, doing things with his neck muscles and arms that were hardly noticeable. "I don't want your promise." He broke off, and abruptly asked, "Which do you think is worse? To tell a lie, or to break a promise?"

I hesitated. I couldn't see what he was driving at. "To break a promise, I guess."

3

"Why?"

"Well, when you give your promise, that means you're bound. You'll do what you say you will."

"So, if you don't promise, you don't have to do it?"

"No. Of course not. I always try to keep my word."

"Then what's the difference?"

I couldn't think of any answer.

"Look at it the other way," he said. "Do you think a person who would tell a lie would hesitate to break a promise?"

"I guess not."

"Then what good is a promise? An honest man doesn't need it, and a liar's promise isn't worth the breath it takes to give it."

"Okay. I don't promise anything."

"I'd like you to ride Fiddler for me next year."

For as long as I could remember Ry had been Joe Fender's jockey. And then Joe died, leaving his wife nothing but a windblown patch of ground and three racehorses. And now Ry had grown too heavy to ride.

I hesitated. "I don't know if I'm ready," I said.

"You'd better be ready," he replied. "In a couple of years you'll be too big." He waited a minute, then he said, "Don't worry about Fetch. I'll tell you how to handle him. Fiddler is ready for this race, and I'll show you exactly how to ride him. Fetch'll never get close to you."

I contemplated telling a lie and saying I wasn't scared of Fetch, but I decided it wasn't necessary; and besides, if I was ever going to start telling fibs, this was not the time. "I never expected this," I said.

He stopped and stood looking at me. "I don't want the Rhal boys to know. If they think it's going to be me riding Fiddler next year, that'll be just fine."

"Do you bet with them?" I asked.

"I don't. My dad used to."

It disappointed me the first time I found out that people bet money on horse races. It was as if the horse

4

alone was not enough, out there in the dust and thunder, running his heart out for them. They needed money to make it interesting, they said. To me that was contemptible. What could be more glorious than that glistening lean body, and those long legs stretching for the wire? This wonderful animal, risking his life for a win, and they're back there calculating odds?

I looked at Fiddler, and he looked at me and nodded his head. He was a big bay with a black mane and tail, and black hooves. His breath had slowed almost to normal, and his hair was starting to dry and curl away from his body. "I don't know if I can hold him," I said.

Ry laughed. "I don't want you to hold him. I want you to point him."

I wasn't trying to talk him out of it. I don't know why I kept coming up with excuses. I said, "Queen of Spades is a running fool." I didn't have to tell Ry that.

"Yeah," he said. "She's going to be tough. But Fiddler is faster—they'll see."

"I can't ride like you."

"You will by the time I get through with you," he said.

I'd never be a jockey, I knew that. I was too big already. But right then my idea of heaven was to be up on Fiddler, and throwing dust in Fetch Rhal's face. "When do we start?" I said.

Ry grinned. "Not till spring. I just wanted to be sure you could do it for me."

"Sure. You can count on me." As he led Fiddler away, he turned and said, "You'd better tell your folks, though. They need to know."

I wasn't sure I wanted to tell my folks. But Ry was giving me good advice—they'd have to know, and it would be better to settle it while it was still in some vague future.

Two

At supper that night I sat there trying to think of how to introduce the subject. I certainly couldn't see any problem with what I was suggesting, but parents seem to have a divining rod for detecting little imaginary land mines in their children's lives. I finally decided not to give it any undue emphasis—that would only raise a flag in my parents' minds. No need for me to be the one to create difficulties where none existed. Finally I said, "I've got a job."

Mother said, "Well, isn't that nice?"

"It won't start till spring, though."

"What sort of job is it?"

"I won't be home from school until late," I said.

"You mean every day?" Mother asked.

"And Saturday, too."

"So who's going to do the chores?" my father asked.

"I'll do them," I replied. "I'll jut be kind of late."

"And the other work? We'll be busy in the spring."

We were always busy. I helped him in the barbershop after school. And as soon as the days were long enough we

7

came home and worked in the garden. "This is really important to me," I said. "It'll only be until July."

Dad looked at me. "Where is this job?"

"It's kind of a secret," I said. "I can't say much about it."

"You'll be needing a security clearance, then."

"It's no big deal," I said. "I just promised I wouldn't tell."

Dad said, "Well, if you're going to work there, you're going to tell your parents where it is. So suit yourself. How much does this job pay? Maybe I'll take it myself."

"Actually, we didn't talk about pay," I said. I hadn't even thought of it. "I don't think there is any pay."

"Just glory?"

"Maybe some."

My dad is a great guy, but sometimes he can be a real pain. "Wonderful!" he said. "Six days a week. Work till dark every night. And no pay. How about the retirement plan?" I keep forgetting that just because I'm excited about something doesn't mean he'll think it's the greatest thing since cheese puffs. I should have taken the time to lay a little groundwork—build up to it, you know.

"I guess I made a mistake," I said. "It's not really a job. It's work experience." Dad looked at me as if I had switched to talking in a foreign language. "Training," I said. "It's very specialized. A real opportunity."

But I couldn't even get Mother on my side. "Ben," she said. 'You really can't expect us to just let you go anywhere to work for anybody at anything."

And Dad said, "You might as well tell us what this is all about."

I guess he's kind of an ordinary-looking guy, but when you get to know him he's a real character. That night, though, he was being especially ordinary. I watched for a glint of the old tomfoolery, but I knew it wasn't there.

8

"Look," I said. "I had no idea this was a federal case." And I knew at once I was off to another bad start. "I'm sorry. It all came up very unexpectedly, and the guy asked me could I keep a secret."

"Guy?" my father said.

"Well, that's part of the secret, isn't it?"

"I don't know," Father said. "He must be asking you to join the CIA."

"How long do you think it will stay a secret in Sweet Willow?" Mother asked.

"I don't know. But I don't want to be the one to give it away."

"And you told him you'd do it?" Mother went on.

"I didn't even think," I said.

"Maybe you should think now," she suggested.

"There's nothing wrong with it," I protested. "This guy just asked me to do him a favor. You know, as a friend."

Dad laughed. "I wish I could find a couple of friends like that. Who is it?"

Mother said, "Surely you can tell us that much."

I thought maybe I could buy them off—you know, if I told them a little bit maybe they'd be satisfied. "It's Ry."

"Ry Fender?" Dad asked.

Mother said, "Well. You can be sure I won't tell anybody."

"And no, I'm sure there won't be any pay," Dad said.

"He talked to me about it," I said. "He's a really nice guy."

"He's just like old Joe," Mother said.

My parents looked at each other. Dad said, "What do you think, Sue?"

Mother hesitated. "I don't know." She didn't want to shoot me down in flames, I guess. "Can you tell us any more about it?"

"I really can't, Mom. But there's nothing wrong with it."

"I just can't imagine what the big secret is," she said.

"You're not supposed to try," I told her. I could see things were going against me, and I tried to think of something to say.

"He doesn't even go to church anymore," Mother said. "And he's old enough, he should be on a mission."

"Maybe he hasn't got the money," I said. "Not everybody goes on a mission."

"Everybody should," Mom replied.

"It's that Lane girl," Dad said. "I can never remember her name."

"Teresa," Mom reminded him.

"Teresa Lane," he went on. He turned to me. "Let that be a lesson to you, Ben. Don't pay any attention to girls until you get home from your mission."

Good advice, maybe, but a little late. But I'd had something on my mind for quite a while, and suddenly I saw a chance to mention it. "It doesn't matter," I said. "I may not be going, anyway."

"What do you mean?" Mom said. "Of course you're going."

And Dad asked, "Why do you say that?"

"Well, I've been thinking about it," I said. "I don't know if I want to go on a mission."

"What has that to do with anything?" Mom asked. "There may be lots of things you don't want to do."

I came up with what I had decided was the unanswerable reply. "Do you think the Lord would want somebody representing him who doesn't want to be there?"

She didn't even hesitate. "What you want doesn't matter," she said. "You do it because it's right. I don't know how you can say such a thing. Here we've been saving the money all these years. What's going to become of the money?"

It was worse than I had thought it would be. "Let's just forget it," I said. "I haven't decided, anyway. It's just that everybody assumes you're going on a mission."

"Of course they do. Why shouldn't they?"

"Maybe you want to make up your own mind."

With a heavy sigh, she let her hands fall into her lap. "I just don't understand you. Why don't you say something, Russ?"

"Leave him alone. He'll be all right."

"Oh, sure. Turn him loose with any riffraff that comes down the pike. He'll be all right."

"That isn't what I said. He'll make the right decision when the time comes."

"Ry isn't riffraff," I said.

Dad replied. "We don't know what Ry is. For all we know, he might have started drinking. Old Joe must have left a few half-empty bottles around."

"He's a good guy," I said. "He's not a renegade."

Mother said, "You see, that's the danger, Russ. He comes across so mild and reasonable."

"That's because that's how he is!" I cried.

"Don't shout at your mother," Dad said.

And Mother went on. "I hope the day never comes when I sit alone in church like his mother. Poor woman."

"The fact is, Ben," Dad said, "he's not the kind of young man we want you spending time with."

Everything was slipping away from me, and I just sat there with my mouth open.

"I know it seems important to you now," Mother said in a reasonable tone of voice. "But in the long run it's nothing. You'll understand that sometime."

"I'll never understand," I said. "And this job isn't nothing. It *is* important."

"It's important to us, too," Dad said.

And Mother observed, "You've never acted like this before. Can't you see he's influencing you already?"

11

Every word I spoke was just digging me in deeper. "Please!" I said. "Don't you trust me?"

"Of course we trust you," Dad said. "I know you have the best intentions in the world, but sometimes intentions aren't enough. You have to remember that your mother and I have been around a lot longer than you; we have watched the influence of friends, both good and bad. When you're a parent, you'll understand."

So I was supposed to put on my Sunday shoes and sit there swinging my feet until I had kids of my own? I even thought about telling them the whole thing about riding Fiddler in the race. But I knew I couldn't do that, and it wouldn't have done any good anyway. My folks didn't care anything about horse racing.

"I want you to tell Ry you can't do it," Dad said.

"How can I? I've already told him I would. What am I supposed to say? Because he doesn't go to church on Sunday, I mustn't get too close to him? I might catch it?"

"Tell him you have too much work to do," Dad said. "Tell him I can't spare you."

"An hour a night?" I suggested. "Maybe that would be enough."

"Far too much," Mother said.

"Just forget it," Dad told me.

Mother became placating. "Things'll work out. You'll see. It's not till spring, anyway." Then she added, "We'll make it up to you, Ben."

Three

Most of the homes in the valley were close to the main road north and south, but not the Fenders'. Joe Fender had not been a main road kind of a man—his life was spent in the byways, looking for things that other men never thought about. So when his father had died and he came into a little piece of property up in the hills, he built a house on it and settled down without a care about what he was going to eat. Even when he married this woman from the next town over, and they had a son, he didn't seem to worry. He kept a few animals around the farm, of course, and tended a garden. But instead of raising sheep, as he could have done, he bought the best mare he could afford and started to breed thoroughbreds. All this my mother told me as she continued to explain my parents' decision.

I had never been to the Fenders' before. I rode my pony across the bridge on the west side of town, and started up the road. As we climbed, the valley seemed to open up under us. I could see all the roads of the town, and cars running this way and that, and the tops of houses, and the full sweep of the river where it hit the bend around Boone Park and then rushed away down the valley.

When I got to the Fenders' I found Ry just coming in from the barn with a bucket of milk. "Hello, Ben."

I got off my pony. "Ry, I need to talk to you."

"Come on in."

In the kitchen, Sister Fender was busy at the stove. She smiled at me. "It's good to see you, Ben."

"Okay, what's up?" Ry said.

I wasn't sure if his mother was in on the secret or not, and I hesitated.

"I can't leave the stove," Sister Fender said. "If you boys have manly man things to talk about, you'll have to go someplace else."

"Oh, Mother," Ry said in a reproving tone of voice. "It's no fun being manly men without a giddy girl around. Quit worrying."

Sister Fender was a small dark woman, intense and restless like her son. She laughed. "Giddy girl?"

Ry laughed as well. "As giddy as we're manly."

"But what about the 'girl' part?" she asked.

"You're the closest we've got."

"It's about riding Fiddler," I said.

"Yes, Ben," Sister Fender said. "I'm so glad. It's wonderful that you can help us."

"The fact is, I can't," I blurted. I glanced at Ry. "My father needs me. He says we're going to be really busy next year." That really sounded lame. I wanted to come up with some story about a big project we would be working on, but we didn't have any such project, and I'd learned that Ry wasn't the kind of guy you tried to sandbag. I'd never even wanted to sandbag anybody before; I wondered what was happening to me.

"I guess I should have spoken to him first," Ry said.

"It wouldn't have done any good," Sister Fender said.

Ry turned to me. "What did you say to him?"

"I had to tell him something," I said. "What I said was I wanted to do a favor for this guy. When he asked me who it was, I told him it was you. That's all I told him."

14

Ry said, "Maybe if I explained what it was about . . . "

"You'd be wasting your breath," his mother replied.

"How can you be so sure?"

"I can tell," Sister Feder said mysteriously. "I'm a mother—I can tell."

"What has that to do with it?"

"I guess you wouldn't know, not being a mother." But she added, "Talk to him if you want."

"All right, I will."

I told Sister Fender good-bye and apologized again. I felt like change for bubble gum, after the way I'd told Ry he could count on me. By the time I got back to my pony he had wandered to the pasture fence and was rubbing noses with Fiddler over the top rail. Ry walked with me. "Looks like Fiddler's found a new friend," he said.

I felt miserable. "I'm sorry, Ry," I said. "I shouldn't have promised."

"Don't worry. It'll work out."

"There are plenty of guys around," I said. "You won't have any trouble finding somebody. That's why I wanted to tell you right away."

"I'm going to talk to your dad."

"He doesn't understand. He doesn't even like horses."

Fiddler's neck was arched as he reached across the fence to nuzzle my pony. He whickered softly, like he was whispering in the pony's ear. I reached to pat his neck, and he rolled his eye at me. I could see myself reflected in that great brown glistening eye. Surely Fiddler and I had a common destiny—winning the Sweet Willow Straddle. I had no doubt that sometime Fiddler would do it; I couldn't think of him doing it without me.

Four

Well, I figured that was the end of it, but some things seem to have a life of their own. That fall, Bishop West hired me to work for him for a week before I went back to school. He needed a couple more men to help brand calves at the community pasture. The other man he hired was Ry Fender. So on Monday night there I was, sprawled on a bunk in the Pine Valley cabin up at the lease, with Ry's bed next to mine, and Toots Latigo next to him, and other cowboys sitting up to play poker, and at the far end Durwood Caswell, Jr., lying on his bunk and staring up at the ceiling. The bishop and the other ranchers and some of the cowboys drove home every night through the week, but the cabin was available, and well stocked with groceries, so some of us decided to spend the nights there. "That's what it's for," the bishop said. My dad had not been keen on the idea, but eventually he gave in. I guess he figured if the bishop was the ramrod, nothing bad could happen to me.

The first night I was lying with my shoulders against the wall so I could see all over the room. The voices of the men rose and fell, criss-crossing each other, occasionally punctuated by a yodel from the poker table, or more often a moan.

Toots Latigo didn't play poker. I don't think his attention span was long enough. As he paced the room, wise-cracking with the men, his eye fell on me. "*Mister Duggan*," he said. "All your life you've been a big nothin', right? But now you're a cowboy."

"Yeah," said one of the card players, as he waited for his hand. "A cowboy. That's a sheepherder with his brains knocked out."

"Not Duggan," Toots insisted. "Duggan has brains he's never used before. Right, Duggan?" He didn't wait for a reply. "On the other hand, he has warts." Toots laughed, but there were only scattered grunts of amusement from the other men. I guess they'd heard all his jokes before.

One of the men said, "You'd better shut up for a while, Toots. You'll sunburn your tonsils."

"Tell us, Duggan," Toots went on. "A highly educated character such as yourself—how do you calculate the area of a circle?"

He was still baiting me, I knew, but I didn't care. The other men didn't respect him any more than I did. "You have to know the radius," I said.

"And if you do know the radius?"

"Then, the area is pi r squared."

Toots swore, and stamped his boots on the floor. "Duggan, how many times I got to tell you, pie are not square. Pie are round." And he laughed again. "You're more fun than a quart of tickles, kid. And I hear tell you're a religious boy, too. Maybe you believe in God?"

"Yes, I do."

"Good for you, kid, 'cause so do I. Do you know why I believe in God? Nobody but God could create a distance as small as the space between Duggan's ears, ain't that right?" When I didn't answer, he continued. "You bet

18

that's right. There's one thing that proves it to me. If anybody but God had made Duggan, he couldn't hear anything; his ears would be touching.''

Somebody laughed.

Toots went right on. "T'other day I see this guy, his ears touched. I asked him how come he was made that way. You know what he said? 'I beg your pardon.' '' Toots laughed again. "He couldn't hear me.''

He laughed like a bouncing ball—starting loud and slow and getting softer and quicker until you couldn't hear him anymore. "Ain't that right, Andy?" Toots called.

Andy didn't even look up from his cards. "Toots," he said. "If you had another brain, it'd die of loneliness.''

I was still mad. "No problem," I said to Andy. "He could get a pet goldfish to keep it company.''

"Oooh!" moaned some of the men in unison before they burst out laughing. And one of them cried, "Better look out, Toots. It bites.''

Toots glared at me, and swore under his breath. Then he strode out through the door and let the screen slap shut behind him.

I looked across at Ry. "He made me mad," I said.

"That's what he was trying to do," Ry told me.

"He's phony as a tin pitchfork," I said. "Where did he get a name like Latigo? Nobody's named Latigo.''

"I think he chose it," Ry said.

"Who gets to choose their name?" I asked.

"Anybody that wants to change it, I guess. Some men wear out their name, and try to hide behind another one.''

"I wish he would hide, somewhere that I could never find him.''

After a few minutes, I said, "I keep thinking about Fiddler. Did you talk to my dad?''

"I tried," Ry said. "But he wasn't listening.''

"With him, horse racing is like face cards—guilty by association.''

"Association with what?''

19

"Gambling, I guess."

"But he lets you ride for other people."

I shrugged. "Maybe it's okay as long as I don't win."

Ry grinned. "That's what I call wicked. Righteousness is running to win." His voice changed. "There's more to it than that, isn't there?"

"What do you mean?"

"Maybe your dad really does need you."

"There's a lot of work around our place," I admitted. "Just because we aren't farmers, people think there's nothing for me to do."

"You know what my mother says?" Ry asked.

"No."

He laughed softly, and looked around the room. The men were involved in their own business—nobody paid any attention to us. "She thinks your folks don't want you spending time with me. They're afraid I'd be a bad influence." He laughed again.

I tried to laugh with him. "Pretty silly, eh?" I said.

"She says if it was the other way around, she wouldn't want her son playing with me, either."

"You're kidding."

"She was kidding. At least I hope she was. I think she was telling me I ought to go to church."

And suddenly, without even thinking, I heard myself say, "It's true."

"What's true? That I ought to go to church?"

"I guess so, but I mean the other part. My folks don't want me to be around you."

He looked like I had slapped him.

"I know it's crazy," I said. "But the only reason is because you don't go to church. Why don't you go to church, Ry? If you did, I don't think we'd have any problem. Why don't you go on a mission?"

"You're serious?" he asked.

"Well, that's what they told me. They didn't want me spending so much time with you, and that's the reason they gave."

"That's crazy," he said.

"I know." Now that I was so deep into this, I decided I might as well keep going. "Why don't you go to church? There must be some reason."

His eyes flashed at me, and then looked down again. "I'll tell you one reason," he said. "One reason is this very thing—this idea that all I need to make me a good man is to go to church. It offends me."

"It shouldn't," I said.

"I'm the same guy, in church or out."

"I don't think you are," I said. "You're different."

"How can you tell?"

He had me there. "I'm sorry," I said. "I guess part of it is, I really want to ride Fiddler. I want my dad to tell me it's all right." I looked across at him. "The other part is, I just don't think what you're doing is right."

"What business is that of yours?"

That stopped me for a minute. Wasn't it my business? I'd never even thought that Ry might not think so. "None, I guess," I said. "Except I want to ride Fiddler."

He was quiet for a few moments. Then he said, "You really don't have any idea what you're talking about. You know that, don't you?"

"No, I don't." I didn't even know what he was talking about.

"It's easy to be gung ho when you're fourteen. I was myself. Everything looks wonderful. Get out of high school, go on a mission, go to college, get a job, get married, have kids . . . There's nothing to it. Well, take it from me, things aren't so simple anymore when you get to be nineteen."

Maybe he didn't remember what it was like to be four-

21

teen. "You know what's right," I said. "You just have to do it." I was starting to sound like my mother.

"Don't you start preaching to me," Ry said. "I've had all of that I can stand. Let's just forget the whole business." He turned over on his bunk.

I was mad. If he wouldn't be so pigheaded, we might be able to work something out on the race. I put all the scorn in my voice that I could muster. "It's Teresa, isn't it?" I said. "You're scared to go on a mission for fear she'll marry old Durwood Junior."

"Hah!"

"It's true, isn't it?" I persisted.

Ry rolled up on his elbow and looked back at me. "Maybe Toots knows what he's talking about. You really are a smart-aleck kind of kid." Again he turned over, with his back to me. "Go to sleep."

What was he talking about, going to sleep? It wasn't late yet. Finally I got up and took a chair where I could watch the men play poker. Among the clandestine books that circulated among the boys my age had been a paperback copy of Hoyle, so I had some idea about how the game was played. I found, though, that watching it was far different from reading about it. The men used familiar words, but their meaning was obscure; well, the profanity was explicit, but it could signify either disgust or elation. The cards seemed to move too swiftly for the eye to follow, and pieces of money crossed the table back and forth like small animals that felt more comfortable in larger packs.

During a pause and stretch one of the men glanced over where Ry lay on his bunk. "Looks like Joe Fender's boy is tuckered out."

"T'ain't surprising," said another. "If I was carrying his load, I'd be wasted, too."

"What d'you mean? He buried his biggest load a couple of years ago."

"Yeah. Well, old Joe is proof of immortality. His body's in the grave, but his debts go on and on."

"But Marge is meeting 'em, so I heard. I don't know how."

"All but one."

"Yeah? What one is that?"

"Durwood Caswell."

"I didn't know he was owin' Durwood."

"Nobody did. He wasn't even talking to Durwood, as far as anybody knew. But I guess one night he got drunk in Lethbridge and Durwood found him. Of course Joe needed money—he always needed money—and it ended up that Durwood gave him a loan; Joe put up his ranch for collateral. Now the note on the loan is coming due."

A high-pitched voice came from the far end of the room. "Goosefeathers!"

The card game stopped where it was, and everybody turned to look. Dur Junior was standing beside his bunk, glaring at them. Dur was about six feet tall, handsome, with palms as soft as Jergens lotion. Nobody could understand why he chose to sleep at the cabin. Maybe it was the only thing he could do to make him feel tough. "Suppose we set the record straight," he said. "You guys are talking about what you don't know about. Dad loaned Joe Fender money, all right, and the reason he did was because nobody else would. If he hadn't, Joe would have lost his place long ago—he'd have died in a ditch."

"Sure, Dur."

Dur muttered, "Anything I can't stand, it's people talking about what they don't know about." He lay down on his bunk again. The card game continued. I went to bed.

Five

Sometime during what seemed like the darkest part of the night, somebody turned on the light in the kitchen and began to rattle the pots and pans. A couple of the fellows yelled at whoever it was to shut up and go back to bed, but the noise only increased. I pulled the blanket over my head and tried to sleep, but the next thing I knew the overhead light came on and Toots' voice shouted, "Rise and shine, me buckaroos!"

Somebody swore.

Another said, "What the blankety-blank time is it, anyway?"

"Five-thirty," came a sleepy reply.

I felt as if it was midnight and I still needed seven more hours of sleep. But I certainly didn't intend to be the tail-wagger on this outfit. I hit the boards with my bare feet, and shivered my way into my shirt and overalls. By the time I'd put on my boots, Ry was sitting up in bed, rubbing his eyes.

Toots appeared in the kitchen door, wearing his hat and pants and underwear. "Rise and shine!" he cried.

He had cooked breakfast, I'll give him that: bacon and eggs and biscuits, fried potatoes, flapjacks, and coffee. He'd even made some cocoa for those of us he called the "Bible-Bullies," Ry and me and a couple of the men. By the time we finished eating and headed for the horse pasture, the pale morning light was just starting to fall across the tops of the timothy.

Last Monday, when the bishop and I had driven to the cabin in his 4X4, we'd pulled a four-horse trailer. One of those horses he had brought for me, and my first job of the day was to catch and saddle him. He wouldn't stand for me, and I finally had to go after him with the lariat. Luckily, I got him on the first loop. Still, he was a good deal bigger than my pony, and the saddle was much heavier than mine. I was aware of mounted cowboys watching me try to lift the saddle high enough. As I stood on tiptoe by that old horse and lifted the saddle toward his back, my arms began to shake. That was bad enough, but then when I finally got it over the hump and it dropped to its proper place—straddling his withers—the cowboys clapped and cheered. I'm sure my ears went red as fireplugs. I buckled the cinch, snapped the martingale in place, and reached for the saddle horn.

Toots Latigo laughed. "Kid. Did you forget to bring your stepladder?"

It sure would have made this easier for me if those cowboys had ridden off to work, instead of wasting all those man-hours watching me get on my horse. But I saw there was no way around it. I could reach the saddle horn, but when I did I was stretched too far to get my foot into the stirrup. So I grabbed one of the saddle strings and kicked my foot as high as I could. It caught, and I climbed. My horse spooked, and started to shy away. I stayed with him. My fingers were locked to that saddle string, and finally I managed to get the horn in my other hand and pull myself astride. By this time my horse was galloping across the field. I had no chance to get my other foot in the stirrup; I was too busy gathering up my reins. But I finally stopped and turned him, and rode back to where the others were getting their assignments.

The fires were going already. There would be men to keep the irons hot, and men to rope the calves and pull them skidding and hopscotching to the fire; others would trip them and hold them down for the iron, and the needle, and the knife, and the pellet. Our job was combing the hills, rounding up the cattle, and bringing them in to the corral—Ry and Dur and me and another cowboy. Most of the day I was working alone. Zigzagging back and forth, I would come in sight of the man on my right, and then the one on my left, and sometimes we'd ride close enough to speak, but for the most part it was just my horse and myself and the hills. Once in a while we'd come across a few head of cattle to catch in our net and crowd toward the corrals.

The first couple of days I was nervous, wondering if I was doing a good enough job. Some of those cows were ornery pelters, and I had a hard time keeping them all together and headed in the same direction. I could tell that Ry and Dur had to wait up for me sometimes. Then I'd start to hurry, and next thing I'd be worrying whether I was leaving any strays in the ravines. But by Wednesday night I began to feel pretty confident.

The men began to accept me, too. They even invited me to play poker. When I declined, a couple of them had to rag me a little. "I bet Joe Smith played poker. What else was he going to do on Saturday night?"

"What's wrong with poker, I wants to know," said another.

"It's gambling, that's what," I said.

"It peers to me the Almighty was taking quite a gamble when he made Adam and Eve. That ain't turned out too good, would you say?"

"It's not the same thing," I said. I glanced toward Ry, but he wouldn't look at me. It was as if he figured I had got myself into hot water, and I could find my own way out.

The fellow explained. "You see, he started out with the dinosaurs, and that was no good. So next it was the saber-toothed tiger. He should have stopped there. That tiger was a lot more useful citizen than a lot of people I know."

Toots said, "Now, you fellas leave Duggan alone. If he wants to believe in Santa Claus and God and the Easter Bunny, what's that to you? Just be sure you talk respectful when you mention them, that's all."

I could take the ribbing of the cowboys—what hurt was the fact that Ry wouldn't help me out. In fact, he'd been awfully quiet all week. He hardly spoke to me anymore.

Six

On Friday morning just after we started work, one of the horses went down in a ravine, and the rider hurt his leg. They couldn't tell if it was broken or not, but the man was in a lot of pain, so Toots put him in the back seat of his car and took him to the hospital in Lethbridge. Just as we were finishing lunch Toots came back and told us the bone had been broken, and they were keeping the man in the hospital for a couple of days.

The work went on as usual for the rest of the day. In the evening the ranchers went home, and the rest of us tended our horses and got washed up. At supper Toots rapped his spoon against his glass to get our attention. "There's something you fellows need to know. I got company coming tonight. If it ain't too much to ask, I'd appreciate you guys trying not to act like orangutans for a change."

"Company?" said one. "Female company, you talking about?"

"No chance of that," another replied. "Latigo ain't as scared of grizzly bears as he is of women."

29

"How come you so scared of women, Latigo? I never see you get close enough to a woman to get bit."

"Shucks, women don't bite Latigo. They stick him with a hatpin to see if he's asleep or not."

Toots growled, "Okay, okay. Have your fun. All I'm telling you is that we got some distinguished guests coming, and it would be nice if you could comb your hair for once."

"Ain't you going to tell us who?"

"It's a surprise."

And he wouldn't say any more. After supper some of the men did change their shirts. Two or three of them shaved, and I saw one down behind his bunk clipping his nose hairs. But after an hour or so the air of expectation receded, and the poker players got out their cards.

"She must be late, Latigo," one man called.

And another said, "Maybe she stood you up."

"Don't get your shirt in a knot," Toots said. "They're coming."

" 'They're coming,' he says," cried another. "You mean there's more'n one? They all coming to see you?"

"They're coming to see all of you," Toots replied.

"You mean there's a whole station wagon full of them?"

"Two," Toots said. "Just two."

The twilight deepened toward dark, and a splatter of rain flew against the window. One of the men cursed. "Now they'll never come at all."

"They're coming," Toots promised.

But the rain fell harder, the darkness closed in, and finally even Toots grew doubtful. "Man, you can't trust nobody anymore," he said. He sat at the window, peering out. "Maybe they got lost," he said.

"We better go look for them. Just imagine, those poor sweet little critters lost in the wind and hail."

There came a knock at the door. "Hsst!" exclaimed Toots. "Here they are." He marched across the room, and when he threw open the door two boys pitched out of the darkness, their faces white as lightning and their eyes like rockets; two boys, almost men, the first all arms and legs and angles, the second as round as a cannon, his wet clothes fitting him like black spandex. They stumbled into the room puffing and blowing, almost falling onto the floor. As they staggered, trying to keep their feet under them, they looked around the room wide-eyed—incredulous, it seemed. Their faces, their hair, their clothes, their feet, were covered with mud. It seemed apparent that they had been caked with dust before the rain started. One thing about them glistened—the small black-and-white nameplates that hung on each breast pocket. I felt a moment of horror—they were missionaries.

Toots stepped forward, and clapped the tall one on the back. "We'd about given you up. Did you have any trouble finding the place?"

The young man smiled. "Boy, Mr. Latigo, am I glad to see you! I thought we were lost for sure."

"You're late," Toots told him.

"Man, you're lucky we're here at all."

The chubby youth said, "You told us it was ten miles."

"Ten or fifteen, I don't know," Toots said.

"From Lethbridge?" one of the cowboys cried. "It's forty miles if it's an inch."

Toots turned with a broad wink. "Forty miles?"

"Well, we made it, anyway," the tall one said.

Toots hooted. "You sure did." He turned to the men in the room. "I want you to meet these two young fellas." He turned, and leaned close to read their nametags. "Elder Somerville and Elder Wiley."

"Ain't that funny?" said one. "They both got the same front name."

31

Toots said, "That ain't your name, is it, Mr. Somerville?"

"No. It's more of a title," the boy replied.

"On account of your age, of course."

"No, sir. On account of my calling as a missionary."

"Oh, you've been called?"

"Yes, sir."

Again, Toots spoke to the whole room. "Men. Today something strange and wonderful happened to me. I was walking down the street in Lethbridge, and I came to these two fellows standing by their bicycles, studying a map. So I stopped to see if I could help them. Well, we got talking, and you know what they told me? They says 'Mister, we are ambassadors of Jesus Christ, and we have a message for you.' And I says 'Oh, yeah?' And they says, 'Yeah. He worries about you all the time.' And I says, 'I ain't surprised.' And they says, 'He loves you.' And I says, 'Well, he's the only one.' " Toots paused and looked at the two elders. "Is that about right?"

"Sort of," Elder Somerville said.

Toots went right on talking. "These boys was ready to save my sinful soul, but I tells 'em not yet. I know guys need it even more'n I do. So they says they'll come out here tonight and save the whole bunkhouseful of us."

"We can't save anybody," Elder Somerville said.

"Oh, did I misapprehend?"

"All we can do is tell you what we believe. You have to decide for yourselves whether it is true."

"How we going to do that?"

"We'll tell you how."

Toots turned to the men. "Hear that? He's gonna tell you how. This is a how-to lecture, boys." Again he looked at Elder Somerville. "Exactly how to *what*? Somethin' went by there so fast I didn't quite recognize it."

The chubby elder's cheeks were shivering. "He's ribbing you," he hissed to his companion.

32

Toots raised his voice. "Anyway, here they are. These fellas have pedalled their bicycles through summer dust and rain and thunder forty miles, and here they are. If you batch of hard-drinkin', card-playin', carousin' sinners don't want to end up in sure 'nough hellfire, you better listen." He waved a hand at the elders.

Elder Wiley leaned close to his tall companion and whispered, "Let's get out of here."

Elder Somerville appeared not to notice. He drew himself erect, and took off his suit coat and vest and hung them over a chair. "Maybe they'll dry a little before we start back." When he turned around to face us his cheeks were still white, and he looked as if he was setting his jaws so his teeth wouldn't chatter.

"They're laughing at us," Elder Wiley hissed. His face was round, and his two front teeth came down between his lips so he looked like a chipmunk.

"Why should't they?" his companion said. "I imagine we look pretty funny." He unzipped his little leather case, took out his scriptures, and opened the Book of Mormon in his hand. The bunkhouse had become very still. He said, "I don't know whether Mr. Latigo intended this as a joke or not . . ."

"Me?" said Toots. "A joke?"

Elder Somerville paid no attention. "It doesn't matter if he was joking. We are not joking. What we have to say to you is serious."

Responses came. "Oh, yeah!" "Say it, brother." "Praise the Lord."

Elder Somerville looked as if he had been slapped. For what seemed like five minutes he stood there, his eyes going from face to face around the bunkhouse as if in search of a friend. I was his friend, couldn't he see? But he hardly looked at me. "I'm sorry," he said at last. "I'm afraid there's been a misunderstanding." He turned and, placing the book back in the case, he zipped it up and began to put on his vest.

33

"Hey!" Toots said. "Where you goin'? You can't stop now."

"We're going home."

Toots laughed. "You can't go home. It's raining."

"I hadn't noticed," the elder replied.

"Shut up, Toots," someone said. "Let's hear what they got to say."

Even the poker players had put down their cards and turned to listen. I couldn't tell if those cowboys were really interested, or if they were just joining in with Toots's little game.

Elder Somerville hesitated. Some of the men actually seemed interested. "What do you say, Elder?" he said to his companion.

"I say let's get out of here," the little elder replied.

The tall one looked slowly around. "What about it, Mr. Latigo? Can you refrain from interrupting us for a minute or two?"

The wind had gone out of Toots's sails. He looked around the room, but nobody was interested in him anymore. "Refrain?" he scoffed. "You know what a refrain is, don't you? That's the end of the song. Well, if you can't tell when your song is over, go ahead. Make a fool of yourself."

Elder Somerville didn't hurry. He stood looking down, and waited for what seemed like a long time. Finally he looked up, and his eyes went around the room, as if to test the attitude of his audience. Presently he said, "When we speak of sacred things, it is important that the Spirit of the Lord be here among us. That is why we would like to begin with a prayer. Is that all right?"

A voice whispered, not in derision, but in solemn warning, "You're gonna need more than prayer."

The elder looked at his companion. "Elder Wiley, will you please offer a word of prayer?"

Elder Wiley looked as if he had been hit in the stomach. But he stepped timidly forward without looking at any

34

of the men, and took a stance with head bowed, feet separated, and hands clasped behind his back. He coughed. When he spoke, his voice was very soft, the words trickling out of his mouth like rain. "Our Father in Heaven," he began. He coughed again. "We thank thee . . ." He seemed to be casting about for something to be thankful for. "We thank thee," he repeated—trying to make it sound more forceful this time—"for the privilege we have of being here." He choked completely. "We ask thee to bless these men." There was a long pause. "Bless them that they will listen tonight, that they may understand . . ." Then abruptly he finished. "In the name of Jesus Christ, amen."

The air inside the cabin changed. They had been ready to give the missionaries a chance, but I suppose Elder Wiley's prayer sounded like a put-down. There was a stir among the men. Someone lit a cigarette. Toots hitched up his trousers, and took a swaggering step forward. "Pretty stingy prayer," he said. "You think anybody way off in heaven can hear a little spit of words like that?"

Elder Somerville had sensed the shifting wind. No doubt he hoped to regain lost ground, but his words sounded weak and apologetic, and what was worse in that company, they sounded as if he were blaming his companion. What he said was, "Elder Wiley just started his mission—got off the bus yesterday."

"And you trust him with a prayer for this passel of polecats?" Toots asked.

I glanced across at Ry, who was lying on his bunk watching. "Why don't they go?" I whispered. I felt as if I couldn't stand any more of this. But Ry didn't reply; I wasn't even sure he heard me.

Elder Somerville was glaring at Toots.

Toots looked back at him. "Well, come on, man. I'm just sitting here on the edge of my chair. Ain't we, boys? This is a voice right out of the thunder and lightning. This is heavy stuff."

35

But the atmosphere was still unpredictable. Someone said, "Shut up, Toots."

Toots cried, "For pete's sake! Can't we have a little fun?"

"Fun?" Elder Somerville asked him.

"It's funny to him," Elder Wiley piped up. "Everything's funny to him. A tee-hee bird in a ha-ha cage."

"Why, you lippy little blimp!" Toots exclaimed. And he rushed at Elder Wiley.

But the tall missionary stood in his way. "We're going," he said. "This time we're really going."

"Going?" Toots cried. "I thought you came here to preach to us. Come on, man. I been waiting for this all day."

Elder Somerville hesitated again. As I watched him I kept saying over and over in my mind, *Go! Get out of here! I can't stand this!*

But he wouldn't give up. "Mr. Latigo," he said. "Do you think you are strong enough to withstand the Lord?"

"I don't have to withstand him," Toots said. "He's a friend of mine."

"Exactly so. Is this any way to treat your friend? To laugh at his messengers?"

"What makes you think he sent you?" Toots said, and laughed. "Look at you."

Elder Somerville said, "No, don't look at us. Listen to us. Will you do that, for just five minutes?"

"I don't have to listen to you. I know what you're going to say. You're going to tell me that Joseph Smith was a prophet. Did you ever hear of the Salamander Letter?"

"The Salamander Letter was a fake."

"Yeah. And so was Joseph Smith."

Elder Somerville turned his back. "All right, Elder Wiley. Let's go."

But Elder Wiley marched up to Toots and said, "How dare you talk like that?"

Toots looked at him. "Listen to it. Man, you're so cute I'd like to take you home with me."

"No chance, mister. Where you're going, I never want to be. But I'm here to tell you, Joseph Smith was a prophet. And President Benson is a prophet today. I know he is."

"You know?" Toots hooted. "Kid, you ain't even figured out why snakes can't walk. You don't know anything."

"And I pity you," Elder Wiley continued. "How can God bless you when you turn his name to cusswords?"

"No thanks," Toots said. "If the way he gives a blessin' is the way he rained on you tonight, I'd just as soon suffer along without."

Elder Somerville had put on his coat, and now he turned shivering to his companion. "Let's go, Elder."

"We got lots of beds," someone said. "You'd better stay with us. It's still raining out there, and darker than the hubs of hell."

"Not as dark as it is in here," Elder Somerville replied.

"We'll be all right," said Elder Wiley.

I wanted to speak—I wanted to stand up and tell Toots Latigo and all the rest, "Listen! Listen to them, you idiots! This is important." But I was afraid. I lay there with my heart pounding in my ears, and didn't say a word, not until the two missionaries had left. Then I whispered to Ry, "Boy, I'm never going on a mission!"

He looked at me. His face was pale, and his eyes wild. With a groan that was almost a shout he flung himself off his bunk, pulled on his boots, and strode out of the door.

"Now, where's he going?" Toots cried. "He want to get soaked to the skin, too?"

"You're crazy as ever, Toots," one of the men said. "It's quit raining."

It had, too. The drumming of the water on the roof had ended, and I hadn't even noticed.

Seven

The next Sunday I was surprised to see Ry sitting in church with his mother. I tried to catch his eye, but he wasn't looking. And when I ran up to him afterward to say hello, he just said "Hi," and kept on walking. Before, he'd always been so full of vinegar he seemed like three people, running around and talking to everyone after church—old people, little kids, it didn't matter. Everybody knew Ry. We were all glad to see him coming back to church, but we didn't understand why he was so different now—so solemn and quiet. But he came the next Sunday, too, and the next, and the next.

And then one day in sacrament meeting, the bishop announced that Ryland Fender had received a mission call to the Colombian Mission. He would leave for the Missionary Training Center on November 15. The whole congregation gave a sigh—we had been afraid that Ry was lost. After church several people clustered around to congratulate him, and scold him for being so quiet about it. He just laughed, and said he hadn't wanted to advertise it—certainly not until it was certain. But presently everybody else was gone, and only Ry and I were standing there.

"You're a sly one," I said. "You could have said something."

"No, I couldn't, Ben. I wasn't that sure it would happen. You know I hadn't been too active, and we had money questions that needed to be figured out."

"I have to tell you, I was surprised." That didn't sound too good. "It seemed to happen so fast . . ."

"I need to talk to you," he said.

We went outside and stood in the snow. Most of the cars had gone home by now; the last few people were leaving the church, or pausing for a final word with friends. Ry made a snowball, and threw it against a telephone post. He hardly ever missed.

"Did your mother know about it?" I said.

"She had to know. We needed to figure out the money." Then he said, "I still need you to ride Fiddler for me."

"Is that the money for your mission?" That sounded like a pretty nervy question, but I felt I needed to know the answer. "The prize money from the race?"

"No. We've been saving the money for years for my mission. But we owe Durwood Caswell."

"What if you don't win the race?"

"Mother and I talked about it. She says it took the two of us years to save this money, and we didn't save it so Durwood could buy a new car. We decided this was the right thing to do."

Again, I couldn't help myself. "You might lose your farm."

"Ben," he said. "You remember that night at the cabin—the night those missionaries came to talk to Toots?"

"I don't s'pose I'll ever forget that."

"I saw those kids—younger than I—that fat little elder; what was his name?" Ry shook his head. "He stood right up there—cold and wet and hungry and forty miles from home—and he looked Toots Latigo in the eye and told him that President Benson is a prophet. Didn't you want to cheer?"

"I sure did," I said.

"So did I."

"Then why didn't you?" I asked. "Why didn't you at least say something, anyway?"

"It was too late. You could see that. Old Toots would have laughed at the Angel Moroni that night."

"Yeah, I guess so."

"I wanted to cheer," he went on. "But I wanted to hide, too. I was ashamed. That should have been me. Those boys had taken my place. They didn't hang back and cry and say maybe later on and worry about whether to get married or not. As soon as they were old enough, they went. What right did I have to sleep in a warm bed and eat all I wanted and never look to the right or the left? That should have been me pedalling my bicycle through the rain and mud. I didn't go to sleep for hours that night, and before I did I made a promise to the Lord. And the next morning when the bishop came to the lease, I took him aside and told him I wanted to go on a mission."

"And I thought you just didn't care anymore," I said.

"I care," he said. "And I still need you to ride that race for me."

"Maybe my folks'll feel different now. I'll talk to them, anyway." I looked up at Ry. "It *was* Teresa, wasn't it?"

He smiled. "I guess so. Partly, anyway. Ben, did you ever have a girlfriend?"

I could feel the color rising in my face. "Plenty," I admitted. "But none of them ever knew about it."

He laughed out loud. "I just feel like there's nobody

else in the world like Teresa. Even the thought of her marrying old Durwood Junior just strangles me. I'd die. I would. But, man, he's sweet on her. And here he is, a partner with his dad now—handsome, rich, a new car."

"Yeah, a Cadillac," I said. "Teresa isn't a Cadillac kind of girl."

"Well, she's sure not a '76 Ranchero kind of girl, either."

"You don't have to worry," I said. "I can tell the way she looks at you."

"Maybe so. But what happens when I'm not here to look at? And old Dur's already home from his mission. He'll have lots of time to wear her down."

I was starting to worry. "So. You're changing your mind. Is that what you're saying?"

"You mean about the mission? Are you kidding? I'm not going through that again. Teresa will just have to wait."

"And she will, too," I told him, as confidently as I could.

"I love her more than I ever did," he said. "But you know something? It'll be all right. I know that now. Whatever happens, it's going to be all right."

"Even if she marries Dur?" I asked.

"Hah! You think I'd want a girl who would be dumb enough to marry Dur?"

"You're kidding me."

"Sure I am. I guess I'm trying to kid myself. But I don't have any choice—it's a chance I've got to take."

So the next morning at breakfast I said, as casually as I could, "Isn't it great that Ry's going on a mission?"

"Well, I'm glad to hear you say so," Dad said.

And Mom added, "I was so proud. I can just imagine how his mother feels."

That remark was for my benefit, I knew. I wished they'd take the pressure off, but I knew it would never happen. I'd never be sure whether I went on a mission because it was really what I wanted to do, or just to make my folks happy.

Mom went on, "Even Joe Fender would have been proud if he could have been there."

"Maybe he was there," Dad said.

"Maybe." Mother's voice sounded as if she wasn't sure if a person of Joe's stripe would be permitted such privileges in the hereafter.

I waited for a while, so they'd think I'd got the message. Then I said, "So Ry won't be here for the race next summer."

"Land sakes, who can worry about next summer on a day like this?" Mom asked.

And Dad said, "I guess old Fetch'll have it all to himself."

My father doesn't have much imagination. He always seems to reach the most obvious solution to a question, and stop. So I thought I'd help him out. I said, "Fiddler can run, whether Ry is here or not. Ry wouldn't ride him anyway; he's too heavy."

Dad glanced at me with a twinkle in his eye. "Do I detect a message here? Could it be that all this talk is leading somewhere?"

"Could be," I replied.

"What are you talking about?" Mother said.

Dad explained. "Your son and heir wants to ride the Fender horse in the Straddle next summer."

Mother had started to clear the dishes, but abruptly she sat down and looked at me. "Oh, dear. I might have known, I guess."

"Well, there's no hurry," Dad said. "There'll be plenty of time to decide next spring."

"But Ry's leaving," I said. "And he has to get me started. You know, introduce me to Fiddler, and show me how to train him. Teach me how to ride the race." I couldn't tell if I'd made my point or not. I'd need all the ammunition I could muster. "And tell me how to handle Fetch Rhal."

"What do you mean by that?" Mother asked.

"Nothing," I said quickly. "Only that Fetch will be the one to beat."

Dad was more direct. "What he means is that Fetch is dirty. He rides to win, and he runs over anybody that gets in the way."

I saw this wasn't going down well with Mother. "He can't run over me until he catches me," I said.

"You mean he cheats," Mother said.

Dad assured her. "If it's necessary. Whatever it takes."

There was a silence.

"You don't mean that he'd hurt another rider?" Mother asked.

"Whatever it takes."

"Well!" Mother huffed. "I should say you are not going to ride that horse."

"Mom!" I exclaimed, then hesitated. I needed to be calm and reasonable. "He'll never catch me. Ry rode against him for years—did he ever get hurt?"

"I don't know."

"Please, Mom. At least don't use that excuse to stop me—that I might get hurt."

"Men have been killed in horse races. I've read about it."

"Men get killed every day—riding bicycles, driving cars, crossing streets. Mom—have you any idea what it's like to ride in a horse race?"

"It's like jumping in a parachute. It doesn't make any sense."

"It's the most exciting thing in the world."

Mom sighed and looked at my father.

"It'll be all right," Dad said. "If he's going to ride, he might as well ride to win."

I could have kissed my dad right then. But I didn't dare move. Mom was sitting there, balanced on her indecision and afraid to fall either one way or the other. I thought about telling her how much Sister Fender needed the money, but I wasn't sure which way that would tip her. At last she reached across the table and took my hand. "You promise to be careful?"

"I promise." *I'll fasten my seat belt; I'll signal at every corner; I won't go over forty-five miles an hour.* I began to worry that she was going to sit there all day, and never answer me.

"All right," she said at last.

And before she could change her mind I had pulled on my coat and cap and gone out of the door.

Eight

I got out my pony and headed for Fenders'. By the time I got there Ry had Fiddler fed and curried and saddled, ready to go. The big bay horse stood in his stall and looked down at me with what seemed like a little smile on his face, as if to ask, *Now, what do you think·you're going to do?*

Ride you, I thought to myself.

"He's got to trust you," Ry said. "You can't be scared."

"I'm not scared," I said.

"There's no need to be," Ry told me. "He's just an old plow horse."

Fiddler was about as much like a plow horse as the Super Chief is like a mule train. I reached up and patted his neck, talking to him all the while, and trying to make my touch firm and authoritative. His nostrils fluttered, and he shifted slightly, his hooves clicking on the cement; I saw white in the corner of his eye.

"He likes you," Ry said.

His head was long and slender, with deep, intelligent eyes, and the skin lying so flat to his nose that you could

47

see the blood vessels under it as clear as rivers on a map of the world. His neck arched upward out of a broad, muscled chest, and beneath it his legs tapered straight down to small black hooves. To me, every line of him seemed perfectly in place, every proportion balanced.

"Can I ride him?" I asked.

"That's what we're here for," Ry said. He had put a western saddle on another horse, and now he led the two of them out of the stable. The fresh air seemed to hit Fiddler like a shot of elixir. He tossed his head and snorted, ready to go. I grabbed his mane and raised one foot behind me, and Ry gave me a leg up. Fiddler shot sideways, almost out from under me, and I had to forget about finding my stirrups until I had reined him in. The trouble was, that took longer than I expected. He seized the bit in his teeth and lunged away. I felt his body surge, and caught a glimpse of the ground flashing under me. It was as if my hands were tangled in the reins, and I was being dragged. I clamped my legs against his sides and pulled with all my might.

"Hold him!" Ry called behind me.

I tried. But his head pushing against the bit only seemed to stretch my arms further as his strides grew steadily longer and faster. Further and further behind me I heard Ry calling, "Hold him! Hold him!"

For a block or two the road was almost level along the hillside, but then it turned at right angles and dropped toward the valley. Fiddler dropped as well—almost a free-fall, it seemed to me. I didn't see how his clattering hooves could keep pace. Surely he was going to fall on his face and break both our necks. But his stiff front legs tried to brake him, sending shock waves up through his shoulders that almost jarred me loose. I forgot about the bridle reins and grabbed both hands full of mane and clung. At last the road turned again and angled downward more gently; and Fiddler, instead of slowing down, flew forward with a rush, as if the race had just begun. With every stride he gave a snort of fear or glory.

At last on the straightaway I was able to find the stirrups. With my boots firmly planted in them I straightened my legs, and taking a short hold on the bridle reins, threw my full weight against Fiddler's bit. At first it didn't seem to have any effect, but I sawed the reins back and forth and jerked them till Fiddler finally got the message. He plunged off the road and up against the fence and stopped. His sides were heaving like an engine, and his breath gushed from his nostrils in noisy bursts. As he bobbed his head and fidgeted, I saw streaks of foam along the bridle straps; his whole body was gleaming black with sweat. I looked over my shoulder and saw Ry coming on the gallop half a mile behind us.

If I'd been a couple of years younger, I would have cried. I knew I'd never get to ride Fiddler again. But when Ry came close he slowed his horse to a walk. I was expecting him to cuss me out. All he said was, "It looks like we've got some work to do."

So until Ry left on his mission, we were out riding every morning as soon as it was light. Gradually I became accustomed to Fiddler, and he to me, so with a touch or a tug I was able to set the pace and hold him there. Ry took me through the race over and over again.

"Fiddler doesn't worry about the start. All that scrambling for position seems to disgust him. He'd rather start slow and run by himself over to one side where he doesn't have to eat dust. Even through the back stretch he's not concerned; just lopes along like an outrider monitoring the race. Try to keep him even with the pack, and don't let anybody get too far ahead of you. Then going into the clubhouse turn, boot him a couple of times. He'll kind of open his eyes and check where all the other horses are, and maybe pick up the pace a little. But then coming into the stretch he seems to lose it completely. He turns into an

49

animal. All you'll have to do is hang on. Let him take the turn wide. He likes to run all by himself, and if you'll give him his head that's where he'll be at the wire—a couple of lengths ahead of everybody, running alone.'' Ry made it sound easy.

But in the next week or so we had a heavy snowfall, and it turned cold. Ry left for Provo to study Spanish and missionary subjects for two months at the Missionary Training Center. The long winter began. This one seemed doubly long to me. Sometimes, sitting in school, I'd look around at the other kids and think how surprised they'd be if they knew I was going to ride Fiddler in the Straddle. When I tried to talk to Mom and Dad about it, they just looked at me with glassy eyes and waited for me to finish. Every few days I rode up to the ranch to say hello to Sister Fender, and make sure Fiddler hadn't forgotten me. A couple of times Teresa was there, too, visiting her. Other than that my life consisted of school and sports and shining the mirrors at the barbershop.

Sometimes Sister Fender would read Ry's letters to me. He said he was getting along well at the MTC, and he'd passed off all the discussions, but he felt he never would speak Spanish well enough to suit him. I always planned how I would write to him and start to get letters of my own, but I never did.

About the first of February Ry phoned his mother one night, because he was leaving for Colombia the next day. They'd arranged it so that Teresa was there at the Fenders', and he got to tell her good-bye, too. I guess it was almost six weeks before anyone heard from him again. At last a letter came. He was doing fine, he said. He had been assigned to Pasto, a small city in the mountains of southern Colombia. His companion was another gringo, but he spoke Spanish very well and he wasn't afraid of work. They were holding more than twenty discussions every week, and had several people committed to baptism. Sister Fender was excited, and I have to admit I was pretty proud myself.

One night a few weeks later I stopped at the grill for a piece of pie, and who should I see sitting in one of the booths but Teresa and Dur Caswell Junior! When she saw me she waved with the tips of her fingers, as if she would be just as happy if I didn't say hello. I thought it must be quite an occasion for Dur to split for a hamburger and fries. He might drive a new Cadillac, but when it came to buying the treats he was tighter than a stuck piston. So I sat there trying to concentrate on my pie, but I kept glancing over toward Teresa and Dur. They looked as if they were sitting in church. Once I saw him lean over and say something to her, and when she smiled back at him it looked as though it hurt her lips. I never saw them say another word.

By that time the snow had begun to melt and the days were getting warm. I brought Fiddler down and kept him in our stable closer to town. And after that I was out in the cool spring mornings, riding the country roads alone. When I'd open the stable door in the morning, he'd look back across his shoulder and greet me with a quiet nicker, and I'd tell him good-day. It was almost as though Fiddler became part human, and I became part horse, and somewhere in between we almost touched.

Every few days on our morning ride we'd climb the hill and stop at Sister Fenders' so she could have a look at Fiddler and know that I was doing my best to get him ready. But she didn't talk about the race. What she talked about was Ry—you'd have thought he was the first missionary on earth. He was doing so well with the language, and he and his companion were teaching so many people, and he wrote to her every week. And she often said, "I wish Joe could have lived to see this day."

At the time I didn't understand. Joe Fender didn't care

anything about the Church—what difference would it make to him to have Ry on a mission? But when I talked to my mother about it, she understood, and explained what Sister Fender's hope had been—that Ry could have filled his father as full of the Spirit as he now was.

Nine

One morning I was sitting on Sister Fender's porch, talking to her, and holding Fiddler's rein, when Bishop West drove up in his 4X4 and stopped with a lurch. As he walked up to the porch, Sister Fender whispered, "I wish he was smiling, Ben." I thought I heard a shiver in her voice.

The bishop took off his hat and stood looking down at it. When he raised his eyes they were full of misery.

"Tell me what it is," she said.

"Marge," he said. "Salt Lake just called . . ."

"What happened?" she asked. "Something's happened, hasn't it? Is Ryland sick?" He didn't answer. "Dead? What?"

"Marge, he's all right . . . As far as we know."

She sank onto a chair, and covered her face with both hands. Now her voice was muffled. "What does that mean?"

"He's been taken hostage," the bishop blurted. "He and his companion."

For an instant she lifted her hands away, her fingers wide apart as if they didn't belong to each other. She looked from the bishop to me and back again, her eyes wide and dry. Then she covered them again, and shook her head into her hands.

"Some masked men," the bishop said. "Last night they stole a city bus and drove it out of town. The police still haven't found the bus, and nobody knows how many people were in it. They estimate eight or ten." The bishop paused. "They think that Ry and his companion were two of them."

She sat without moving or making a sound. Presently she said, still speaking into her hands, "They think?"

The bishop quietly explained as much as he could. "It happened near the missionary apartment. Six missionaries live there, as you know, and of course when Ry and his companion didn't come home the other elders reported it. The police decided they must have been on the bus."

"Who did it?"

"They don't know who they were, or what they want, or anything. They are waiting to be contacted."

She burst out, "They're just sitting there, waiting?"

"Of course not. They're doing everything they can. The president has been informed, and the embassy is working on it."

"Thank you, Bishop." It was spoken like a dismissal.

"Of course. If there's anything I can do . . ." The bishop turned. "There may be some publicity."

"Yes." She wouldn't look up from her hands, though as yet I couldn't tell that she had started to cry.

After the bishop left I just sat there. I couldn't think of anything to say.

Sister Fender shook her head, still holding her face in her hands.

"Shall I go home?" I asked.

"No, Ben. Please. Stay. I don't know . . ." Her voice was soft and feathery. "Do you think there might be a mistake?"

54

"There has to be a mistake," I said. "Any number of things could have happened."

"Yes." She lowered her hands and looked at me. "Some of them don't sound too wonderful, either, do they?"

"Don't worry," I said. "Ry can take care of himself." The words may have sounded brave and confident, but I realized that my voice certainly didn't. The words were nonsense, anyway. It wasn't going to do Sister Fender any good for me to act as if nothing was the matter. "I'm sorry," I said. The truth is, I was scared. I couldn't even imagine where Ry might be, or what it must be like to be kidnapped by bandits.

"Maybe you'd better go, Ben," Sister Fender said. "I think I'd like to be alone."

"Sure," I said. I didn't know whether to give her a hug, or what to do. But she looked as if she might break if I touched her. "See you soon," I said. And I got on Fiddler and rode away.

Ten

That afternoon a couple of newspaper reporters and a TV mobile unit arrived in town, and that night Ry and Sweet Willow were on the network news. By the next afternoon the whole world knew what Ry liked for breakfast, and that he planned to be a doctor. We all had a chance to tell everything we remembered about Ryland Fender. As the days passed, the furor started to die down, and not a moment too soon to stop Marge Fender from committing some mayhem against the media. There was still no indication who the abductors were, or what they were trying to achieve. Diplomatic efforts to solve the puzzle continued, we were assured.

Then one day a letter arrived at the post office for Sister Fender—a letter from Ry. The postmaster called our house and said she probably wouldn't be in for the mail until tomorrow, so would I like to take it up to her? I certainly would. Fiddler needed a workout, anyway.

When she opened the door she had a book of scripture in her hand. "Ben, I can't do anything," she said, even before I was in the house. "I can't go outside and work. I can't work inside, either. Look at my house. I've never

seen such a mess. Come on in. I can't cook myself anything, and when I do I can't eat it. I can't do anything but
think about Ryland, and I can't stand to do that, either. I
can't even read my scriptures. I'm turning into a basket
case."

I was digging into my shirt pocket. "You've got a letter
from him," I said. "Maybe everything's okay."

"Oh, Ben!"

I handed it to her. She stared at it as if it was a bomb.

"Go ahead and open it," I said.

"I'm afraid to." She looked closely at the postmark. "I
can't tell when it was posted."

"Do you want me to do it?" I asked.

"No, no. I'll do it." She took a deep breath and tore
the letter open. After a glance at it, she said, "No. It was
written before. The same day, I guess."

Life slowly turned back to run in its old familiar chan-
nels, except that sometimes I would be aware of a great
cavity inside me, which I recognized as fear for Ry. Or if I
had no other reminder, there were my visits to his mother.
She reached a sort of plateau where at least she could func-
tion—the house grew neater than I had ever seen it. But
though she tried to reveal no evidence of concern, I could
never look at her without remembering the dread she lived
with.

Weeks passed. The media quickly lost interest in the
story, and even the people in Sweet Willow went back to
their normal routines. I understood their feelings. It was
hard to know what to say when you met Sister Fender. If
you asked about Ry, it might remind her of her sorrow
during the only minute of the day when she had been able
to forget it. If you didn't ask her about Ry, she might think
you callous and unfeeling. Nor was it any easier for her to
know how to speak, I'm sure. As the days went by, she
began to retreat, growing more and more subdued and un-

communicative. How many ways are there to say "No, I haven't heard anything"? Sometimes it seemed that it would never end, and we would live out our lives and never know what had happened to Ry. More and more when I went to the Fenders', Teresa was there, too.

One day Sister Fender said to me, "Ben, I know it's a lack of faith. The ward had a special fast, and we all prayed together for Ryland—and, I'm sure, alone. And there hasn't been a minute pass that I haven't sent up a prayer that he would be safe; even that we would hear something—whatever it was. Do you think after all that, that the Lord can be unaware of what's happening? That in the course of his busy day he has somehow missed the fact that he has a son in trouble? Of course not. He's not old and deaf. He could hear that pounding on the door.

"So the question is, why doesn't he answer?" She looked at me as if she expected me to know.

"I guess sometimes we have to wait our turn," I said, and thought at the time that it was a pretty stupid remark.

"Nonsense!" she said. "In a good average minute, how many prayers do you think are on their way to heaven? Thousands? Millions? Maybe billions, for all I know. If we have to wait our turn, how long would it take? A hundred years, every time we got down on our knees? No, Ben. You don't just take a number, and wait, or stand in a long line of people winding up through the stratosphere. He answers each prayer at the same time—at the time it's offered. 'Yes,' or 'No,' or 'Maybe later.' But he answers it. So we must assume that he has answered ours. The answer hasn't been yes or no, so it must have been later. Well, Ben, I've waited as long as I can. If Ryland is dead, I've got to know it. If he is still alive, I want to know where, and in what condition. So, you may ask, how am I going to find that out? The Lord's going to tell me, that's how. When I convince him that I'm really serious, he'll tell me."

I wondered if the strain had been too much — if maybe Sister Fender's mind was slipping.

"Tomorrow morning I'm going to fast and pray, Ben. And I'm not going to eat again until I get some word."

She meant it. I started wishing I'd never come. I even began to feel out of patience with her. At last I said, "Why do you tell me about it?" So I would join in her fast? I couldn't. The thought scared the daylights out of me.

"I have to tell somebody," she said. "If I don't know that somebody's watching me, I might not have the nerve to finish."

"You'd starve yourself to death?" I asked.

"Fasting and starvation are not the same thing. When you fast your body grows weak, but your spirit gets stronger. When you starve, everything dies."

"It's a crazy thing to do, even to think about."

"Not really," she said, and smiled at me. "And I'm not going to die, not yet." As I left the house, she said, "Ben, I know you're concerned about Ryland, just as I am. But this is something I want to do alone, do you understand? You've helped enough, and I want to do this alone."

It made me feel funny to realize she thought I would fast with her. I had no intention of it. I looked back at her. "I know you won't die, because I won't let you."

She followed me to the door, and as I got on Fiddler she called, "I need your faith, Ben. Not your doubt. I have enough doubt of my own."

I reined Fiddler around to face the house. She looked so small and frail standing there in the doorway. "I'll pray with you," I said. And then I added, "It's going to be all right."

After that I rode up to the ranch quite often. I guess I expected to see her growing more and more desperate, and becoming pale and weak. But she surprised me. She was cheerful as always, more relaxed than I had seen her since

Ry was kidnapped. She scolded me. "Don't fret that way, Ben. You said yourself it's going to be all right."

I wished I could believe that; I really did. I wanted to have faith, but it wouldn't come. The situation was hard for me because now I had to worry about both Ry and his mother. I mean, if she died, it would be my fault. I knew I couldn't let that happen. Yet at what point did I break her confidence and tell the bishop? I worried about it day and night. I had no time or energy for faith.

But for Sister Fender it was as if Ry was already home by the fire. She went about her work around the farm, singing to herself, and once I even saw her hopscotch like a little kid. From time to time she'd take a drink of water. But I could tell she was getting weaker.

"This can't go on," I said.

"Tut," she told me. "You have to quit worrying. Don't you remember the three steps to solving a problem?"

"I give up." I was really out of patience with her. How could she go on acting so cheerful, when every minute she was dying?

She explained. "Number one: You pray about it." She looked at me as if to ask if I knew the rest.

"Okay. I'd say we have not neglected number one."

"Number two: You do everything you can."

"There's nothing we can do."

"Exactly. Number three: Don't worry."

"I can't help but worry," I said. "And there is one thing we can do. We can fix you a plate of dinner."

"That's not going to solve the problem."

"It'd solve half of it."

She laughed, but even her laugh had grown frail. "No, Ben. You mustn't worry."

"You have to have some nourishment," I said. "Look, even Mahatma Gandhi drank fruit juice."

"No, Ben. Water's fine. All fruit juice does is drag it out. Tell me some way to make the time shorter."

"Well, at least you could be grouchy. It isn't fitting to smile at a time like this."

"I feel fine. Really, I do. After the first day, it hasn't been hard."

It was almost grotesque. Obviously her brain was suffering from malnutrition.

One time when I got there, Sister Fender was asleep, but Teresa was sitting in the kitchen reading a magazine. "I don't know what to do," she whispered. "Sometimes I wonder if I should be fasting, too. His mother doesn't love him any more than I do. What's the matter with me, Ben?"

"There's nothing the matter with you. What you and I can do is pray."

"I've prayed till I'm blue in the face. Do you think he's all right, Ben? Are we ever going to see him again?"

"Sure," I said. "One of these days we'll get a letter and find out that he's the president of Colombia."

"How can you joke about it?" she said.

On about the third day I got a phone call after school. It was the postmaster. "Ben? There's a letter here for Sister Fender."

"From Ry?" I cried.

"I wondered if you might like to take it up to her."

I was out of the door almost before the phone was in the cradle. But halfway to the stable I stopped. Slowly I turned and walked back into the house and went to my bedroom and closed the door. I just stood there for a minute, feeling as if my heart had swollen and choked off my windpipe and was still growing bigger. Two thoughts tumbled over and over in my head. First, that it had worked—that the Lord had honored Sister Fender's faith. And second, that Ry must be all right.

I knelt by my bed and tried to say a prayer, but my

62

mind wouldn't hold still. It kept running off like a wild horse, and then it would hit the end of the rope and I'd have to drag it back. Yet even while it bucked and yahooed it was really saying, *Thank you for Ry, and for his mother. And thank you for not letting my doubt get in the way. I'll never doubt again.* Even while I thought that, I knew it wasn't true. There'd probably come other times of doubt and discouragement about many things, but as far as prayer is concerned, I knew then that God hears us. And when he can, he helps us.

My whole skin was jumping like a jazz band; I couldn't wait any longer. I knew that by then the Lord knew I was grateful. I shot out of the room and out of the house and down to the stable and off to the post office, riding Fiddler. The letter was a small, thin envelope carrying a Colombian stamp. The address was in Ry's handwriting. I couldn't believe it. I don't mean that I had doubted, exactly, but having that letter in my hands was like holding the surety of God.

The road to the Fender ranch had never seemed so long. If I could have let Fiddler run all the way it wouldn't have taken many minutes to get there, but an uphill run for several miles is not the approved way to train a racehorse. So we loafed along, and I passed the time by marvelling at the letter in my pocket, and wondering what it said.

I arrived at the Fenders' just as if it was any other day. When Sister Fender heard me come in the door she called from the living room, "Ben?"

"It's me." I didn't know how to break this to her, and I stopped in the kitchen.

"I've decided this is the life," she continued. "Do you realize how much time we spend cooking anc' cleaning up? It isn't worth it. I haven't washed a dish for days, and it's heavenly. I'm never going to eat again."

"Wrong," I said.

"What do you mean, 'wrong'?"

"I mean you are going to eat again." I opened her refrigerator.

She came in from the living room, and stood in the doorway, watching me.

"Now, let's see," I said. "What have we got?"

"I want to know what you're up to, Ben. Are you ragging me?" I gave her what I hoped was an innocent look. "You are, aren't you?" She caught her breath. "What is it? Don't, Ben. I can't stand it."

I closed the refrigerator door. "Maybe you'd better sit down," I said.

She put her knuckle between her teeth, and backed onto a chair. Her eyes were as round as buttons on an overcoat.

I took the letter out of my pocket, and handed it to her. She looked at it, and then up at me. "Is it real?"

"Well, I'm not the one that forged it, I promise you."

She raised the letter and looked at it again, as if it took ten minutes to read the address. "Oh, Ben. I'm going to cry." And she did. The tears sprang up in her eyes, and she choked and tried to hold them back.

"Let go," I said. "It's not a sin."

A little smile flashed across her lips, and then suddenly she put both hands up to her face and doubled over, sobbing. She looked like a little girl crying on the playground, and I wanted to kneel down and put my arms around her. But I just leaned against the cupboard and waited. It didn't take long. She was too anxious to open her letter to spend much time crying, and soon she was tearing at the flap and pulling out the slip of paper. "May 11," she said. "Oh, Ben. He's alive."

She read silently for a moment; then she looked up at me. "He's alive, Ben. He's all right. Do you want to hear it?"

I shrugged. "Well, now, I don't know why you'd think that."

She laughed. "Silly." She held up the page, and started to read:

>   This is going to be short. If Baby Fat catches me writing, he'll have my skin. I'm all right. Elder Jensen and I were part of a busload of people when the bandits drove off with us. We don't know where we are or who they are or what they want. Our guard is a little kid—well, he has a mustache, but he looks as if he was born with it. He's a feisty little pelter, though. He says he'll mail a letter for us, and you'll know whether he did or not if you ever get this. Ha, ha. If Baby Fat catches him doing us any favors, he'll be dead meat. I guess this is a pretty dumb letter, but I just want you to know we're okay. I'll try to write more later. My comp's folks are Clarence and Ida Jensen and they live in Cheyenne, Wyoming. Area Code 307, 638-3378. If you get this letter, will you please call them and tell them Glen is okay?
>
>   We have not forgotten who we are, and the gospel is still true. I love you, Mother. Hope you are okay.   Ryland.

"He's written a postscript," Sister Fender said. "Look." She handed me the letter. " 'Say hi to Ben.' "

Of course she phoned the Jensens. But she wouldn't have needed to. Within a day the whole country knew about the letter. Mail came in from all over, as people shared their concern with Sister Fender. That helped, of course, but that wasn't what she needed most.

Eleven

One day I was walking down the street when I saw Durwood Caswell, Sr., coming toward me. He was a tall man, very straight, and walked as if he was still a soldier. He'd won the Distinguished Flying Cross during the war. From what I'd seen, and what I'd heard people say, it seemed that nobody liked him very much, but everybody was nice to him because they owed him money. I pitied him. If that's the only way you can make friends, what use are they?

But he did cut an imposing figure, and I never saw him when he wasn't wearing a three-piece suit. As we drew near, I could feel his eyes fingering me. Then all at once he stopped, and leaned back with a little smile on his face. "Good morning, Ben."

I was surprised that he knew my name. I said quickly, "Good morning, sir," and immediately wanted to kick myself. Why did I call him "sir"? I never called anybody else that. I saw that the legendary charm, or flat intimidation, or whatever it was that Durwood Caswell was said to possess, was more real than I had imagined. I braced myself against it.

67

"I'm Mr. Caswell," he said. "Maybe you know that."

"Yes, sir." There. I'd done it again. This guy was creepy. I would have known him better, you see, but he never came to the barbershop. His head was as slick as an eight-day clock. I guess that's why he always wore a hat.

His face still crimped with his odd little smile, he said, "I'm told that you will be riding Mrs. Fender's horse in the race this summer."

"That's right," I said. The secret, for whatever it was worth, had gotten out long ago.

"Fetch Rhal beat him last year."

"Ry was too heavy." Again I scolded myself. I didn't owe this guy any explanations.

"Maybe. Maybe the horse is just not good enough."

"Fiddler's good enough," I said. "You'll see. Fetch Rhal will be lucky to find the finish line."

Durwood Caswell's smile opened by about another millimeter. "You want to bet?"

"I don't bet," I told him. "Especially on horse races."

"Where's Marge Fender getting her entrance fee?"

"That's Mrs. Fender's business."

He reached to put his hand on my shoulder, but I backed away. "What are you so jumpy about?" he asked. "You may not know it, but I'm your friend."

"I've got plenty of friends."

"Ahh," he said. "But can they do what has to be done?" Then he asked me, "Would you like an ice-cream cone?"

Of course I wanted an ice-cream cone, but I had money in my pocket. I didn't have to accept the invitation of Durwood Caswell. Still, I had no reason to antagonize him. I followed him into the shop and we took our cones out and sat on a bench in the sun. I licked my ice cream and tried to figure out how he operated. He was leading me around as if he had a ring in my nose.

68

"How much is Marge Fender paying you to ride?" he asked.

I couldn't believe this guy, and I couldn't believe myself, either. Why I should spend two minutes with someone as rude and pushy as him, I couldn't understand.

"Perhaps I'd better explain," he said. "These questions of mine are not just conversation. I have an interest in the result of this race. You probably know I loaned Joe Fender some money before he died."

"Everybody knows it," I said. "And they know how much."

"Well, it wasn't as much as it will take to pay me back. My point is that if Marge doesn't win that race, I don't know how she'll ever pay me."

"Yeah," I said. "Too bad. Then you'd have to take her farm."

"Nonsense," he said. "Who told you that?"

"Everybody knows it. Isn't that why you loan money? So people can't pay, and then you get the farm?"

His lips actually broke apart, and he laughed. "Is that what you think?"

"It's true, isn't it?"

"I loan people money to help them. And I never loan it to them unless I think they can pay. But sometimes they won't pay, or can't, as in the case of Joe Fender. What do you think I ought to do in such a case?"

"Give them time."

"Okay. The Fender payment is due next fall. How much time shall I give her?"

"Just don't go after her now. How can she think about your money at a time like this?"

"Exactly. Now, if we can win this race . . ."

"We?" I asked.

"There may be something I could do to help."

I couldn't believe this guy. Mr. Fix-it. You got a problem, he can fix it. For a fee, of course. The only problem was, I didn't have a problem. "Yeah. Well, I'll give you a call."

"Of course you're right," he said. "If she doesn't win the race, I'll have to do something."

"You may be able to help," I said. "Do you own a bowling alley?"

"What's that got to do with it?"

"Oh, just an idea. Something she said."

"Don't get smart with me, kid," he huffed. "You just tell her what she's up against, will you? I hate dunning widows."

"She's going to pay you," I said.

"Sure. They're all going to pay me. I should live so long. Kid, what do you know about it? How long do you think I'd be in business if I didn't collect my accounts? I try to be nice to people, but they act as though I ought to be a combination of the Red Cross and the Salvation Army. I'm a businessman."

I got up from the bench. "Thanks for the ice cream."

"Let's talk about the race," he continued. "What's your strategy?" He stood up, too, towering over me.

I don't know. Maybe I had him figured wrong; maybe he was only trying to help. But his manner set me off—I couldn't even be polite. "Speaking of strategy," I said. "How are you going to persuade Teresa to marry Dur?"

He snorted, and seemed about to blow some steam at me. But he checked himself. "I'm sure Teresa is able to decide for herself who she wants to marry."

"You bet she is," I said. I walked on down the street. What was he trying to do? I felt uncomfortable, as if I'd barely escaped some kind of marriage—to a person I didn't even know.

Twelve

One morning I was out on Fiddler when I saw Fetch Rhal riding toward me on Queen of Spades. I was just going to ride by him, but when he stopped in front of me I knew that wasn't going to work. I stopped as well, and looked at him.

Fetch sat in his saddle like a churlish imp, with one shoulder down and one eyebrow raised. When you first looked at him you thought he was smiling, but then as you watched you weren't so sure. He said, "I guess you're riding for Joe Fender."

"Joe Fender's dead," I reminded him.

"His widder, then."

"It's Ry," I said. "He's the one I'm riding for."

"You're wasting your time," he said. "You got any sense, you'll let that poor old horse rest, and you'll stay home and get your sleep."

I didn't like the look of Queen of Spades. She moved so smoothly her joints must have been as slick as oil. I was immediately ashamed, feeling as if I had been disloyal to Fiddler, and I said, "Oh, I don't know. Fiddler almost beat her last year, and he was carrying a hundred and forty pounds.''

He laughed. "Yeah. She was just a colt. She's a year bigger now, and a year smarter, too. Poor Fiddler's just older and stiffer.''

"You're scared," I said.

"Hey, man, I'm cool." He shrugged. "Just passing the time of day. Hate to see a bright kid like you waste all that time and miss all that sleep for nothing.''

I urged Fiddler past him and on down the road.

But instead of riding on as I had expected, Fetch turned his horse and followed me. Finally I looked back to see what he was up to. He was riding along two lengths behind me, just sitting there on his horse, one shoulder down and one eyebrow up, and that half smile still on his lips.

I leaned forward and nudged Fiddler with my heels, so he started to trot. Out of the tail of my eye I saw Fetch give Queen a flip with his quirt, and she leaped forward, but he pulled her back till she was trotting close behind us and slightly to one side. It was a dirt road, soft after the rain, but with two smooth tracks down it where the car tires ran. Queen was in one track, Fiddler in the other.

Queen was a fidgety beast, and she was snorting and grunting as she trotted along, which didn't do anything to settle Fiddler's nerves. I knew his nerves were a little frayed, because he kept turning his head slightly with his eye rolled back to see where Queen was and what she was up to. He trotted faster; Queen, too. He broke into a gallop; Queen, too. She stayed right with us, huffing and snorting so close behind us I fancied I could feel the spray from her nostrils.

Little by little Fiddler lengthened his stride. You could pick up the variation in pace by the increasing rhythm of the hooves thudding on the earth—faster, faster, faster. I didn't like what was happening, but I didn't know what to do about it. I took a glimpse back at Fetch, still sitting there smiling, his big brown hands straining against the tug of the reins. He was laughing at me.

I could have stopped Fiddler, perhaps, and let Fetch ride on alone, but the truth is I was afraid to try. If I wasn't strong enough to stop him, Fetch would really have something to laugh about. Meanwhile he had started to inch up on us, which spooked Fiddler all the more, so he tried to pull away, but the mare ran even faster. Almost before I knew it the two horses were running flat out, side by side. I gave up any thought of controlling Fiddler. I leaned forward as far over his neck as I could, and held the reins tight and even. Fetch was still smiling.

But gradually the quirky curl in his lips straightened. The solemn fact was that Fiddler was pulling ahead. Fetch lashed the mare with his quirt a time or two, but she was already stretched to her limit, and still slipping back. I laughed out loud.

It was more than Fetch could stand. If he had stayed in there, who knows what might have happened down the road a mile or so? But Fetch wasn't willing to take the chance. He reared back in the stirrups and jerked on the reins, and before she had even slowed properly he spun Queen around like she was a quarter horse and started back the way they had come.

With his competition gone Fiddler began to slow down, and at last I reined him in and walked him back to the stable. If Fetch had been trying to prove something, I doubt if he hit the mark he was after. But he may have learned something, too, and looking back I realized I'd have been better off if he had never got smart.

Thirteen

The next week another letter arrived, and I took it up to Sister Fender's. This one was fat with pages, and she opened it as if she was lifting the lid on a treasure chest. "Look at it, Ben," she breathed, holding the sheaf of paper in her hands. "Looks like friend Ryland must have written himself a novel. Have you got time to stay and listen to it?"

"If you don't mind," I said. I'm nervous listening to other people's mail if they haven't had a chance to read it first. What if the writer suddenly starts to make some horrible confession? But of course, what would Ry have to confess, anyway?

"I need someone to talk to when I'm happy," she said.

Sure. As long as the letter continued to make her happy. You know how sometimes words rush right out of your mouth, and before they're past your lips you know you should never have let them go? It happened to me then. I said, "As long as it's good news."

She looked up at me with a start. *What is he trying to do?* her eyes seemed to say. *Ruin my one moment of hope?*

I wanted to tell her no, I was just a stupid crazy kid that ought to be locked up where he couldn't talk to anybody, much less to a widow woman whose son had been captured by bandits. But I couldn't say a word; I couldn't even leave. I just sat there with misery clogging my throat, and waited for her to speak.

"It doesn't matter," she said. "They say that good news is doubled if you share it, and bad news is cut in half. Either way, I need you here."

"I was kidding," I said. "It has to be good news. If he wasn't healthy, he couldn't write a letter that long. And if he wasn't alive, he couldn't write a letter at all." And as soon as I'd said it, I squirmed again, and put a mental fist in my mouth.

"Listen," she said, and she began to read:

Dear Mother:

Yup, we're still alive and kicking. Hoping you are the same, ha, ha. You remember Ramon, our little jailer? Did you get my other letter? Anyway, Ramon has become our friend, sort of. He has smuggled in some paper and pencils and pens and stuff, and he promises to mail our letters. So we'll see.

I guess the first thing is to try to tell you what has happened. Maybe you know all about it, I don't know. Maybe the people on the outside know more about what's happening than we do in here.

It's not exactly the Hilton, so don't let them kid you about that. They're holding us in this big old house miles back in the jungle. I guess there used to be a plantation here. We don't have any furniture in the room, and the floor gets kind of hard sometimes. The bad news first. The bad news is that the food isn't great. The good news is that there isn't much of it.

Never mind. We're surviving. For only one reason, though. On that crazy bus ride, when the only thing I could think about was grabbing hold of anything solid and hanging on, Elder Jensen was already fighting back. He opened his scriptures, wrapped the Bible around his left ankle and his triple around his right ankle, and stretched his socks over them to hold them in place. So when we got to the house and the guards frisked us, they missed the books. If we have any sanity left, it's because we've had those scriptures to read to each other. Whenever we hear Ramon unlocking the door, we hide them in the fireplace.

Ramon is a comandante in the body of a boy. You should see him strut. He's only about five feet tall, but he stretches his neck so high he almost leaves the floor. He has this horrible, scraggly mustache and beard, and black banjo eyes. Basically, he would look pretty repulsive if it wasn't for the glow on his face—it shines like an angel.

At first he tried to be really tough with us, but as the time passed and we got to know each other, he began to soften. He even mailed that other letter to you, he says. That doesn't seem like much, maybe, but around here it's the kind of thing that could cost him his neck. These guys are so paranoid they shoot at a dripping faucet—or they would if the faucets in this house would drip. They won't even run.

One day Ramon told us that El Oso was coming. He was awestruck. He spoke so reverently, you'd have thought it was the Second Coming. For the next few days, the whole house crackled with expectation. Women were brought in to wash the guards' clothes and clean the house. We could peek through the vines and see the men down in the courtyard, cleaning their guns and making their bullets shine.

On the appointed day three jeeps loaded with mock-military bandits drove into the yard. We were watching from the window. A young man threw his leg over the side of the jeep and stepped down onto the ground, carefully holding himself at attention all the while. Compared with the others, he looked splendid. His uniform was without a wrinkle, his decorations winked in the sun, and his boots shone like silver. Our fat captain almost tripped over himself, fawning and saluting.

El Oso scarcely noticed him—he was studying every detail of the property.

First, he asked to see the hostages—all of them except Elder Jensen and me, as we had been separated from the others since we arrived at the house. When they were brought before him, he hissed, "Idiots!" He was not speaking to the hostages. "These are not hostages." He turned to the captain. "Have you been feeding this riffraff?"

The poor captain tried to stand at attention, but his stomach remained at ease. "Only beans, my comandante," he said. "And very little of that."

El Oso snorted. "They never had it so good. Did any of them try to escape? No, of course not. They hope you will keep them forever. And that is what you will have to do if you are waiting for a ransom. Who is going to pay you to release these wretches? Nobody. Let them go."

As soon as the captain could collect himself and give the command, the hostages vanished into the jungle.

"Now," said El Oso. "Where are the others?" We could hear the whole battalion thunder up the stairs, escorting their distinguished leader. Our door was unlocked and opened, and El Oso himself stepped into our room.

"So?" he said. "These are the zealots. Why do

you come here?" He walked around us. "You think you can tell us about God? For two thousand years we have been worshipping the same God in the same way. What have you to tell us?" He was slapping his riding crop against his boot. "Why don't you speak? Have you no tongues in your head?" He continued his slow parade around and around us. "Your government has deserted you. This church for which you have sacrificed so much cares nothing for you. You are fools!"

He turned to the captain. "Search the room!" You should have seen the poor captain. He looked around. There was no furniture, no carpets, no drapes—where could anything be hidden? Still, he gave the command and his soldiers fanned across the room, pretending to search the cracks in the floor. But finally, of course, one looked in the fireplace and found the scriptures, which he handed to the captain, who in turn passed them to his superior. El Oso accepted them with a satisfied smile on his face. Without a word he turned toward us, and threw the books on the floor, then tramped on them with his heavy military boots, grinding his heel into the pages. Apparently satisfied at last, he strode to the door and glanced back at the captain. "Burn them," he said. Before the captain could speak, Ramon stepped forward, gathered up the torn and scattered pages, and took them out.

But a few days later when he brought us our supper, we noticed that he was unusually quiet. He sat and watched us eat, and presently he said, "What is this book?" He held up his shirt, and we saw the remnants of the Book of Mormon tucked in his belt.

"Didn't you burn it?" I asked.

He replied, "While the Bible was burning, I opened this and began to read." He took it out of his belt and looked down at the book as if to start reading again. "What does it mean?"

Elder Jensen replied, "It means, Ramon, that the Lord has placed this book in your hands."

He looked at us in wonder, almost in fear. "Why would he do that?"

"Because he knows that you are prepared to read it."

"Yes. I have read it."

"All of it?"

"No. Not all of it."

At that moment we heard another guard at the door, and Ramon quickly covered the book with his shirt. it is like that here; we never know when we will be interrupted.

Sister Fender turned the page over. "That's all. It's not even signed."

I smiled. "Now, how will we ever find out who it's from?"

She couldn't help smiling, too. "Okay, okay. I won't complain. But I don't know whether I feel better or worse."

"Of course you do," I said. "He's alive, he's still feisty. You've got to feel better."

"You're right," she admitted. "He is feisty; I do feel better. I just think of what he's going through."

"It's going to be all right."

"Oh, Ben. Do you think so?"

"How can he lose? Those clowns are no match for that kind of gumption."

"But the letter just ends. Suppose they caught him writing it?"

"You know Ramon has to pick up the mail when he can. Would you rather Ry mail it off, or wait till next week sometime, after he had a chance to sign it?"

She sighed. "All right, already. If you insist. I feel great."

Fourteen

About a week before July 24, I got up one morning to take Fiddler for his workout. As I stepped out the door I noticed that the pasture gate was down, and my pony had run away. Then, when I turned toward the stable, my heart lurched. The door stood open. I ran to look; the stall was open, too. Fiddler was gone.

Dad took me in the car, and we looked up and down the streets of the town. We found the pony, and I rode him home. By the time I got back to the house, Dad had returned, too. He had scoured the countryside and not seen Fiddler.

I spent the entire day riding my pony up and down the roadways and pastures and backyards around Sweet Willow. I double-checked every horse I saw. I had seen a movie once about a bay racehorse that some tricksters had painted black to conceal his identity, but it would take more than a coat of paint to disguise Fiddler. I stopped frequently to scour the hills with binoculars. No Fiddler. Just before dark I rode up to the Fender place. Sister Fender came out on the porch. "How are you, Ben?"

"All right, I guess."

"You look as if somebody beat you with a stick. And your pony's tail is dragging a mile behind you."

"There's something I have to tell you," I said.

"Not Ryland?"

"No. Nothing about Ry." Not directly, anyway. I couldn't think of any diplomatic way to say it. "Fiddler is gone."

"What do you mean, gone?"

"Lost or stolen, I don't know. Last night somebody opened his stable door, and this morning he's gone."

She sank onto an old wooden chair she kept on the porch. "You think somebody did it?"

"The gate was down, too. Somebody had to do it."

"Do you think it was the Rhals?"

"I don't know. Anybody could have done it."

"I think it was the Rhals," she said.

"So do I."

"Come in, Ben. Have you had supper?"

"No. I ought to be getting home."

"I'll call your mother. She can spare you for an hour."

I tied up my pony, and as I came into the kitchen Sister Fender was just hanging up the phone. "She says it'll be all right." She set another place at the table, and I pulled up a chair.

"Durwood Caswell was over here yesterday," she said.

"What did he want?"

"He wants his money."

"Yeah," I said. "He wanted me to talk to you about it. I guess I forgot."

"He was just reminding me, he told me with a smile."

I felt uneasy. I wasn't used to people talking to me about grown-up problems. "That's some smile he's got, isn't it?" I said.

"I guess I could pay him with the money we saved for Ry's mission." She pretended to laugh. "As long as those bandits keep him, he doesn't need any money, anyway. Free room and board, free entertainment, free transportation; such a deal." She broke off nervously. "I guess what was in the back of our minds was that if we were doing the Lord's work, he wouldn't let us lose the farm. Maybe I believe that, I don't know. But doing the Lord's work is no guarantee. Did it save the Prophet Joseph Smith from trouble? I guess God wants us to have a little faith in ourselves, too."

I couldn't help saying, "Maybe deep down you had faith in the race; faith in Fiddler."

She almost laughed. "I wonder." She turned away from me. "I guess that's what you call justice, isn't it? You start to put your hopes in a silly horse race, and somebody steals the horse."

"We'll get him back," I said.

"Maybe." She rose, and went to the window. "You know, Ben, I don't know what I'd do without this old farm. It's nothing but work, and it's full of painful memories, and an angel himself couldn't make a living from it, but it's home, you know what I mean? And as long as I work like a slave I know I'll have something to eat. What am I ever going to do if I lose it? Move to town and learn how to type?" She shook her head. "I don't know." She returned to her chair and settled back, staring at me across the table. "But I'll tell you something. I'll do that if I have to. I'll take in washing; I'll scrub floors; I'll sell real estate. I don't care. My life's going right on, and when Ryland comes home he may find me living in one room over a bowling alley. But he's never going to hear me cry."

"We'll get him back," I repeated.

"I know that," she said, with a shiver in her voice. "I've never doubted it for a minute." She misunderstood me; she thought I was talking about Ry.

Fifteen

That night I sneaked out of my bedroom window and went to the pasture to catch my pony. He looked at me out of the darkness, and gave a little whiffle of surprise, but didn't object when I slipped the bridle rein around his neck. "We've got a little job to do," I whispered. I led him back to the stable and put on the saddle, and headed for the edge of town. As soon as we were beyond the last house I kicked him into a gallop.

The night was indigo as to color, but powder as to texture. I mean that there were no hard edges; everything seemed suffused, as if I was on one side of a fine screen, and the world was on the other. Even the rim of the half-moon was blurred. Yet the air felt clean and fresh, and I breathed it in as if it were strengthening medicine.

When we were about a half mile from the Rhals' ranch, I pulled the pony back to a walk again. I was not crowded for time, but stealth was very important. With that in mind, I had tried to prepare in every way I could think of. In one pocket I had a penlight, and in the other some meat scraps wrapped in foil.

At the main gate I tied the pony to a post and continued on foot. The ranch buildings lay massive and dark against the pale hill, and except for the frogs and crickets, as quiet as a paper cutout. I walked up the dirt road, and at a Y turned off toward the barn. It was a huge structure, built back in the days when horses provided the power to run the farm, and even in the darkness evidence of decay was obvious—old paint, broken windows, loose boards. Still, it stood proudly silhouetted against the sky, its three cupolas standing straight, the center one topped by a weather vane in the figure of a trotting horse.

Just as I reached to slide the barn door back, a dog barked somewhere. I jumped as if he had bit me, and turned. The single bark erupted into a chorus, and I saw a tangle of dark forms coming toward me, yodelling. I grabbed the foil package out of my pocket, and tried to unwrap it, but I couldn't find the edge. The scramble of carolling hounds came nearer and nearer. At last, in a final desperate gesture, I ripped open the package and threw it in the face of the closest dog. The charging animals turned in upon themselves, and the barks faded to faint, gluttonous whines and yips, and then to snarls as snapping teeth tore the package to shreds and fought for a piece of the prize.

I entered the barn, and slid the door closed behind me. The interior smelled of horses and old hay, and I heard the click of hooves, but it was too close and dark to see anything but the faint grey window lights.

I turned on my penlight. It seemed to illuminate the interior of the barn about as much as one star would brighten the sky. But when I shone the feeble light down the length of the barn, its reflection was caught in several horses' eyes, which glowed dull red like dying coals. Hooves clicked, and quiet nickers drifted through the darkness. I started to hurry down the wide center aisle of the barn, shining my light into each stall as I passed. Most of the stalls were empty. In only a moment, it seemed, I had reached the far end of the barn, and come up with a feeling of disappointment and uneasiness. If the Rhals had kidnapped Fiddler, where would they keep him except inside their barn? But if they had not taken him, who had? I heard a sound from beyond the wall in the end of the barn, and shone my light in that direction. I realized it was not an outside wall, but had been built after the barn was finished to create a separate room in the end of the building—a grain bin, maybe, or an office. I found the door, and opened it.

There were two box stalls in the end of the building, and from one of them came a nervous whinny and quick flurry of hooves on cement. It must be Fiddler, I thought, but the door was too high for me to see. I turned a grain bucket upside down, and, standing on it, shone my light into the stall. The horse was Queen of Spades.

I heard a sound behind me, and spun my light around. There, standing in the door I had just come through, was Eli Rhal. He had pulled his pants on over his underwear, and slipped his boots on. His face was grizzled with yesterday's whiskers; his hair stood above his head as white as feathers.

"Who is it?" he asked.

"Ben Duggan," I said.

"What, the Duggan kid? You down here hunting Queen? What you going to do to her?"

"No, I . . ."

"You're feedin' her something, right? Make her sick. You're scared to race her fair and square."

"I'm looking for Fiddler," I said.

"Fiddler? Well, he ain't here."

"He's disappeared."

"What you talkin' about?"

"Somebody took him out of the stable."

Eli laughed. "And you think it was me?"

"Nobody else cares. All the rest of them are running for third place. They know that the race is between you and me."

He said, "You're daft, kid."

"He's gone. Somebody took him." I got down off the grain bucket. I was still almost as tall as Eli. Folks say that Fetch got his pint size from his dad, and Trooper his walrus size from his mother.

He said, "What kind of win is it, if you have to cheat to do it?"

"I'd never cheat!" I cried.

He took the light out of my hand and shone it up and down my body, and then held it on my face. I turned away, blinded.

"Neither would I," Eli said. Then, with elaborate patience he continued, "Kid, you have to pay attention. You get careless and leave the door open, what do you expect?"

I couldn't tell if he was sandbagging me. *Did Fetch tell him about our impromptu little race?* I wondered. I wasn't going to do any good tonight, I saw that. I started toward the door. Eli went ahead of me and opened it, and the hounds rushed in, yodelling. Eli motioned to me, and we slipped out, and he quickly slid the door closed. The dogs rushed against it, their voices angry now that he had tricked them.

Eli said, "Kid. I ever catch you in my barn again, I'll let 'em have you. You hear what I'm sayin'? About three bites, and there'd be nothin' left but shoelaces."

I didn't answer, and I didn't look back. I walked to my pony, and mounted, and started for home, the anxious voices of the dogs fading behind me.

Sixteen

A few days later, another envelope from Colombia arrived at the post office. By now it was almost a ritual for me to deliver the letter, and for Sister Fender to read it to me.

Dear Mother:

Are you all right? One of the hardest things about being stuck here is wondering what's happening at home. The race is coming up next week. Is Fiddler ready, and Ben? Have you seen Teresa? I wrote to her, too. In case she didn't get the letters, tell her I'm okay.

I don't think this can go on much longer here. I know they'd like to be rid of us, but they're afraid to let us go. Baby Fat (that's what we call the captain) thinks we know too much. The truth is, we don't know anything. But they're scared.

On the other hand, they think if they kill us it'll bring a landing by the U.S. Marines. I'm sure El Oso doesn't think that, but he is miles away, and has other concerns. Meanwhile, poor Baby Fat is left to figure out what to do with us. After all, he's the one that captured us in the first place. Every day his disposition seems to get worse.

It is a good thing we have Ramon. He got some blankets for us, and every day he tries to smuggle in some of the leftovers from their meals. If it weren't for that, we'd probably have starved by now on the swill Baby Fat sends us.

But—are you ready for this? We are giving Ramon the discussions. He rescued our Book of Mormon from the fire, you know, and started to read it. As soon as we got a chance, we asked him what he thought about it. He told us, "What I have read, I believe."

"Yes. Because it is true."

Ramon hesitated. "What shall I do?"

"Continue to read."

"Is that all?"

"No. We will teach you. And when we are free, we will baptize you."

He looked at Elder Jensen. "You would never baptize me—a murderer."

"Have you ever killed anyone?"

He hesitated, as if he were ashamed. "No. Not yet."

"And now you never will."

It was not a simple matter, teaching Ramon, of course. There were several other guards coming and going all the time, suspicious of each other, and anxious to curry favor with their captain. So when Ramon came into our room he would shout at us angrily for the other guards to hear, and then we would whisper to him the sweet truths of salvation. We prayed with him, and talked and worshipped with him. And we found that in this situation—where, if the captain found out what we were doing, he would surely kill us—the gospel became to each one of us far sweeter than it had ever been.

One night when everybody was asleep, Ramon crept into our room with a candle, took the book from under his jacket, and carefully arranged its tattered pages. "I was just reading in the fourteenth chapter of Alma," he said. And suddenly he gripped the book in his hand and raised it in front of us. "Do you believe this book is true?" he asked.

"Shh," I said.

He was so excited, he could hardly keep from shouting. "Do you?" he repeated.

"Of course," I said.

And Elder Jensen added, "Yes. I know it is true."

Ramon moved closer. "Let me tell you a story about two missionaries in prison. They were bound with cords, their food was taken away, their water, even their clothes. The judges and lawyers visited them day after day, questioning them and hitting them and spitting on them. But they said nothing. The judges threatened them with death, and still they said nothing. And finally one day the judges and lawyers came again and shouted at them, and struck them, and spit on them. And this time Alma spoke—not to the judges, but to God. And do you know what he said? He said . . . Here, let me read it to you.

" 'How long shall we suffer these great afflictions, O Lord? O Lord, give us strength according to our faith which is in Christ, even unto deliverance. And they broke the cords with which they were bound; and when the people saw this, they began to flee, for the fear of destruction had come upon them.' "

Ramon looked up from his book. "But they were too late. There was an earthquake, and they were all so frightened that they lost their strength and fell on the floor. And the earth shook, and the walls of the prison came tumbling down and killed them. Only Alma and Amulek were left alive, and they walked out of the prison and were not hurt." Then Ramon asked us, "What are you waiting for?"

"What do you mean?" I said. I was afraid that I already knew.

"Is your faith less than theirs?" Ramon asked. "Does God love you less?"

And Elder Jensen gasped—he did. He literally gasped. "You want us to ask for an earthquake?"

"I want you to ask for deliverance."

"You know we have prayed," Elder Jensen said. "You have prayed with us."

"Don't *ask* him," Ramon insisted, pointing toward the sky. "*Tell* him. Tell him out loud, like Alma did."

I was ashamed. I wanted to stand up and call down the Lord's deliverance, as Alma did, but I couldn't. If you can imagine, I thought to myself, *What if it doesn't work? What will that do to Ramon's testimony?* I looked at my companion, and he looked as if he was frozen. Neither one of us had the faith to ask for an earthquake—even for deliverance. And before we could get control of ourselves, Ramon strode angrily out of the room. Though he still brings us our meals, for the last two days he has hardly spoken to us. I don't know if he will mail this letter for me or not.

Sister Fender looked up from the letter. "Apparently he did."

"Is that all?" I asked. "Isn't it signed?"

She smiled. "It's signed, all right. With an affectionate little note to his mother."

92

Suddenly I felt lighthearted. "It's going to be okay. Don't you think so?"

But she was still looking down at her letter. "They say that death is no big deal," she whispered. "The only thing that matters is how we live, not how long. But sometimes, death sure does seem like a big deal."

Seventeen

A storm front moved in that evening, and it started to rain. This wasn't just your smiling little raindrops hurrying down out of the clouds to dampen the daisies—this was Niagara Falls, a mile thick and forty miles long. A steady roar droned on the roof all night, and when morning came we left the lights turned on; the sun could not seem to get through the dark fury of the storm. All day it poured, and all night, and into the next day again. There were respites, when the dark sky would brighten a little and the rain slow to a patter, but these intervals only seemed to give the storm a chance to draw breath and return with new frenzy a few minutes later. People were out in their raincoats and rubber boots, ditching their yards and piling things up in their garages. Some were pumping out their basements; some even bailing with buckets.

Work in the area came to a sloshing halt. People were concerned with only one thing; if they didn't have rescue missions of their own, they helped their neighbors. The post office remained open because that was the law, and the general store because people were constantly coming in for shovels or gunnysacks, garden hose, rubber boots, gloves and raincoats, and hot chocolate. Most other businesses closed; school was out for the summer, and whole families were out in the yards, battling in any way they could the ever-rising water.

On Sunday evening the storm passed. Hearing it go was like standing on a railway platform when the train pulls out. You feel buried in the furious din of the machine, and then its last car passes you with a rush, and the whole screeching chorus of wheels and engine and rattling cars slowly fades down the valley until it disappears. That night when the sun went down, we could see the stars.

The next morning everyone was out assessing the damage—fences down, sheds floated away, livestock gone, yards gutted, basements full, trash littering the land. The most awesome thing was the thing we couldn't even see —the bridge on the west side of town. It was gone completely. The hurtling grey water that had carried it away still flowed level with the river banks. But the sun was so bright and the day so warm that within a couple of hours someone remembered that today was the day of the race. The thought seemed laughable. A little later, though, as people worked to repair the damage, someone else expressed the thought that everybody needed a little fun. Why not run the race, mud or no? The horse enthusiasts caught up the idea. By midmorning the race committee had gone into informal session around a large culvert in the middle of town. The culvert had become plugged, and had created a pond that covered the main street for a quarter of a mile. The committee, consisting of three of the town's most dignified gentlemen, supervised the unplugging activities while they discussed the question of holding the race. Witnesses gathered to testify pro and con. Many people thought it was unconscionable to troop off to the racetrack when there was so much work to be done. Others argued that people were tired, and needed some diversion.

Then they could go back to work with new vigor. ". . . Just because your horse ain't a mudder . . ." But then someone said, "Looks to me like we're going to have a race."

Everybody looked up to see Eli Rhal's truck cross the intersection at the end of the block, pulling a horse trailer. He turned the next corner, and headed for the track.

"That settles it. If you let him, old Rhal will run that race all by himself, and claim he won it."

"We'd better start drying that track off, or you won't have anything but duck races."

The crowd dispersed, some directly to the track; the rest went home to get cleaned up.

While I was home, I tried to phone Sister Fender. Even though we didn't have a horse to enter, she'd probably be wondering whether or not they were going to have the race. But her line was dead. As I sat there by the phone, my dad said, "Are you riding today?"

"Frank Downey wants me to ride for him," I said.

"Well, aren't you going to?"

"I don't know. I really don't feel like it. And his kid can ride as good as I can."

"You know that isn't true," Dad said. When I looked up in surprise, he continued, "You're the best jockey in town; everybody wants you."

This didn't sound like my dad talking. He'd never wanted me to ride before—he thought it was dangerous, and silly besides, when I didn't even get paid for it. But I didn't care about being paid. If I had to, I'd have paid them to let me ride their horses. But that day was different. I'd worked so hard and planned so long to ride Fiddler that I felt I couldn't accept a substitute. Today, I couldn't stand to see Fetch Rhal's upside-down face at the clubhouse turn again, grinning back at me from under his armpit. I wanted to splatter Fetch with mud—Fiddler's mud. I wanted to take that check up to Marge Fender and tell her the farm was safe. And now none of it was going to happen, and I felt sick. I thought maybe I wouldn't even go down to the track, but in the end, of course, I couldn't stay away.

Once preparations for the race were started, everybody got on the bandwagon. Someone swept dry the seats in the grandstand; the refreshment committee straightened up the lemonade booth and festooned it with red and white crepe paper; they even used the leftover paper to brighten up the judge's stand. The sound sytem was set up. The tractors chugged steadily around the track, their harrows tumbling the mud to dry it out. Somebody brought a pump to drain a long puddle of water that covered the back-stretch, but the ground remained wet, the top six inches about as thick as cream of wheat.

At first the talk had been of just staging the derby, but as the day progressed and the sun grew warm and the word spread, contestants in all categories showed up, ready to ride.

There would be a pony race, an old-timers' race, a wagon race, a quarter-mile race, a relay race . . . The event of the day, other than the derby, was a challenge match between a new tractor and an old 1925 car. It looked like a full afternoon, and as the people kept coming, and trailers rolled in one after another with their horses, and the announcer growled a welcome into the microphone, I began to get excited.

The first race was for the old-timers—you had to be over sixty to ride in it. If their joints were stiff, though, they didn't show it. They came loping out onto the track like a bunch of schoolboys, waving their caps, their bright shirts fluttering in the sunlight. I half expected a band to start playing. But after the race, when the horses trotted back toward the grandstand, they were all the same color— mud—the horses, the saddles, and the riders, their faces swollen like grotesque black masks. I don't know how they saw where they were going.

A voice said behind me, "Ben!" I turned to see Frankie Burns, a pale ten-year-old kid who couldn't care less about a horse race. His days were spent in his room lying amid stacks of comic books. Now he was puffing, and trying to push his bike, whose wheels were caked with mud. "Where's the bishop?" he cried.

I tried to talk him into leaning his bike against the grandstand. If he could hardly push it, he didn't have to worry about anyone riding off on it. Still, he wouldn't leave it. He said it was brand new, almost.

"Bishop!" he shouted when he saw him, and tried to speed up. "Bishop! The president called Sister Fender!"

The bishop turned. "What is it, Frankie?"

"Annie asked me if I'd tell you. She has a call from the president for Sister Fender, but her line's dead."

"President?" the bishop asked.

"The president of the United States!" Frankie cried. "He wants to talk to her."

Eighteen

The bishop frowned. "Frankie! What are you talking about?"

"It's the truth, Bishop. Annie says so, anyway. It's the president himself."

The bishop modulated his voice. A small crowd had begun to gather. "Just tell me the message."

"Fenders' phone is out!" Frankie cried, louder than ever. He was starting to feel quite important. "And the president wants to talk to her."

"It must be about Ry," somebody said.

"Of course," the bishop said. "Why didn't I think of that?"

"It's dead as a doornail!" Frankie announced. "Her line, I mean."

"Maybe she's here," said the bishop, looking around.

"I've been watching for her," I told him. "I don't think she came."

"Did the president say what he wanted?"

"He didn't say anything, I don't think," Frankie said. "Except he wants to talk to her."

Somebody said, "That must be good news."

"Yeah." The bishop's voice grew quiet again. "Or bad. I'll go get her." He started off toward his 4X4.

Following, I said, "Can I go with you?"

He turned. "You'll miss the race."

"I'd like to come."

"Sure. Come on."

We got in the four-by, and he drove sixty miles an hour through the town—must have been throwing mud a hundred yards. But at the river he jammed on his brakes, and the truck slewed to a stop, sideways in the road. The river was roaring like a freight train. One timber of the bridge still lay at an angle, half under the water. Everything else had been washed away.

"Now what are we going to do?" cried the bishop.

"We can make it," I said. I had no idea whether we could—I just knew we had to get to Fenders' place.

"Get out, Ben," the bishop said.

"I'm going with you," I insisted.

"No, you're not. I don't want your neck on my conscience, 'specially if I'm drowned dead."

"We can make it!" I cried.

His expression changed. "Ben. Do as I tell you."

I got out of the four-by, and stood back to watch. I was mad. I'd be glad when I was old enough that I didn't have to take orders from anyone.

With is head and elbow hanging out of the window, he started slowly forward. The front wheels of the four-by dipped into the water at the edge of the stream, and then moved downward. I kept waiting for it to level off, but it didn't; just kept going down, down, down. Before the top of the hood went under water, the front wheels rose a little, and seemed to level off. Maybe that was as deep as it would go. If so, it might be all right—the truck was moving steadily through the water. But then it dipped again. I thought I saw it tip. The bishop looked back at me, and all

102

of sudden the color was completely gone from his face. He shouted something I couldn't understand, and then repeated it. He waved me away. "Get help!" Was that what he was saying?

As the four-by continued, one front wheel rose a little; just enough, it seemed, to give the force of the water a chance to get under it. The whole outfit seemed to rise, and then it tipped onto its left side, carrying the bishop down with it. His head appeared in the passenger window, which was now facing the sky. He waved again, and tried to say something, but started to cough. The truck turned again, caught by the furious rush of the stream, and tumbled two or three times, rather fitfully, until it came to rest with only its tires showing, splaying the grey water back upon itself in showers of foam. I stood, unable to move. Was the bishop trapped inside the cab, was he crushed beneath it, or was he already hurtling downstream, caught in the torrent? And what could I do? I was the one who had urged him to try it. Maybe if I had said nothing he would have tried some other way to reach the Fenders' place. Was it all my fault? I was willing to plunge into the water if I could have done any good, but I knew that nobody could swim against that current.

But at that moment I saw his blue shirt emerge from the water and then roll beneath it again, slightly downstream from the overturned truck. I ran along the bank. Then I saw his arm, and his hand at the end of it grasping at the air. His face appeared, eyes wide and mouth open, and then was swallowed up again. If only I had a lariat, or wings, or if only I could go back five minutes in time . . .

The stream was carrying the bishop so fast that I could hardly keep up, though I ran as fast as I could. His face was out of the water, and under and out again, his arms pulling strongly against the current. Then suddenly he stopped. He had hit something; perhaps a remnant of the bridge that had gotten jammed against the far side of the river.

The bishop was flattened against some invisible stanchion with the water pouring around him, but he was able after a moment or two to raise himself high enough to hold his face out of the water. There he lay for some time. I knew I ought to go for help, but I wanted to be able to report. Report what? The point at which he disappeared for the last time? There was nothing I could do for him. But then, slowly, he inched his way up the thing that had caught him, and finally dragged himself out onto the grass of the river bank.

I turned and ran back to our house. I got on my pony and rode him to the racetrack. As soon as I told the men what had happened they began to jump into their cars and their pickups, with their winches and lariats, and drive away toward the river. But I rode north of town, heading toward another bridge six miles upstream. Then, as I passed the school, I saw the footbridge across the river. It was a simple suspension bridge, high enough above the water that the logs and debris that had taken out the big bridge had flowed harmlessly beneath this one. My pony was nervous, but I urged him gently, and finally managed to lead him over the bridge, which until now had felt nothing but the feet of children.

Once I was on the other side of the river, I headed for the Fenders' in as straight a line as I could follow. I opened gates and cut across fields, and in one place where the wires were slack I pulled a post and dropped the fence flat and led the pony, shivering, across it.

My unaccustomed route took me across parts of two or three different ranches, one of which belonged to Durwood Caswell. In the middle of the land stood an abandoned homestead, marked by a clump of willow trees and an old swaybacked barn. The house had been moved away long ago and the road to the place plowed under. It was like an island in the great sea of rolling meadow grass. Cutting through that field on my way to the Fenders' place, I came within a couple of hundred yards of the barn. And just as we were passing it I heard a shrill whinny. I stopped my pony. He pricked his ears toward the barn, then stretched his neck and neighed. Another whinny. Fiddler! I'd know him anywhere. We turned, and galloped to the homestead.

The place was lonely—ghostly even, absolutely still except for the hollow whisper of the wind stirring the leaves of the willows. I got down from the saddle and started to walk through the tall grass. As I approached the barn, the impatient, high-pitched whinny sounded again, so loud I almost jumped. The barn door was gone, and I saw the flash of Fiddler's eyes in the dark interior, and heard his nervous whicker as he shifted back and forth inside his stall. The air was no longer fresh and blowing when I entered the barn, but musty, so close and still it seemed to have been unchanged since the day the first load of hay was unloaded into the loft. I patted Fiddler's shoulder, and he looked back at me with a quiet murmur.

"I'll be back," I told him. "You wait right here." And I hurried back to my pony.

Nineteen

Within a few minutes I rode up and stopped my horse in front of Fenders' place. Sister Fender saw me, and came out on the porch. "Ben," she said. "I didn't expect to see you today. Is the race over?"

"It hasn't started," I said. And then I added, "I'm going to ride for you."

"Don't tease me, Ben."

"I found Fiddler," I said. "Just now. He's in the old barn on the Parkman place—you know, where Durwood runs his cattle."

"Well, what are you doing here, then?"

"I want you there to see it."

"Then let's hurry."

I hadn't actually forgotten what I came for; I was afraid to mention it, I guess. "There's something else," I said.

She had started into the house, but turned at the door. "Couldn't it wait?"

"Not this."

I was still sitting on my pony at the gate. She looked at me from only a few feet away. She didn't change a hair. "Ryland?" she whispered.

"I don't know. I think so."

"What do you mean?"

"The president wants to speak to you on the phone."

"What president?"

She knew what president. But I said, "The president of the United States."

It took her a minute to answer. "What does it mean?"

"I don't know."

"My goodness." Again she turned toward the house and stopped. "Do you have to wear your Sunday dress to talk to the president?"

"I don't think he cares."

"I guess I ought to comb my hair, at least." Still she hesitated. "Why did they send you up here on a horse?"

"The bridge is out."

She hurried into the house. She was not gone long, but when she came out she had changed into a pretty blue dress and combed her hair, and even put some makeup on. "Do I look all right?"

"You look great. I wish he could see you."

"Can you imagine being on the network news in bib overalls?" she asked.

She had a point, I guess, but I don't understand these things. It wouldn't have bothered me.

She opened the car door. "Well, let's go. You can get your horse later."

"I'm going to get Fiddler."

"Never mind that now. We've got to see what this call is all about."

"Maybe there's still time, though, to make the race."

"Good night!" she cried, and burst out laughing. "I'd forgotten all about the race."

"I'll be there as soon as I can," I said.

She rolled down the car window, and I saw that there were tears in her eyes. "Ben. I can't stand it."

"It's going to be all right."

She tried to laugh again. "Just as well I didn't put on any mascara."

"You'll have to cross on the footbridge," I said. "Leave your car there, and walk."

"I wish I could fly." She drove quickly away.

I rode as fast as the pony would go down the hill to the old barn. My first thought had been to change the saddle to Fiddler, and ride him on into town, but I wanted him fresh and full of vinegar when we got there. So I put my lariat over his head, threw a half hitch around his nose, and let him down across the meadows. He didn't think much of the idea of crossing three strands of barbed wire laid flat against the ground, but finally he danced across, catching the corner of his fetlock and making the wire sing. He lunged like he was headed for Toronto, but I was able to hold him with the hard lariat loop on his nose. We travelled on. Even when the pony was going at a hard gallop, Fiddler glided behind him at a trot.

When we got to the footbridge, Sister Fender's car was parked there. She could walk on into town, but the bridge presented problems for me. It was narrow, with railings on either side, and swayed slightly even when little kids walked across it. Add to that the roaring grey water only a few feet below it, and it was a scary situation for anybody. For a creature the size of Fiddler it looked impossible. As I tried to lead him onto it he hung back, with head high and nostrils fluttering. I insisted, but Fiddler didn't care. I pulled, chattered, cajoled, begged. Finally, feeling desperate, I yanked the rope. Fiddler reared back with a snort, and his eyes rolled.

I didn't know what to do. Maybe if I led the pony ahead of him, he'd follow. But I couldn't control both of them. Then, as Fiddler twisted his head anxiously against the rope, I had a thought. He was scared, like a horse in a fire. They say that the only way to get a horse out of a fire is to blindfold him.

I let up on the rope, and led Fiddler away from the edge of the river, patting his neck, whispering to him, trying to calm him down. I took off my windbreaker and slid it over his neck. Slowly then, little by little, I moved it forward over his ears, down to cover his eyes. He stood trembling; his nostrils buzzed with apprehension. I tied the arms of the windbreaker under his throat, and tucked the corners in carefully so that he couldn't see anything. I spent another minute or two trying to calm him down again. He was far from reassured. He still stood on legs as stiff as posts, quivering. But I had lost all the time I could spare.

I took hold of the rope just under his chin, and led him in a circle around the grass, first one way and then the other. He seemed to be settling down a little, though his breath still came in nervous, vibrant puffs. The thing I needed was to become more confident myself. Boldly I led him back across the grass, turned and walked straight onto the bridge. When his hoof first touched the boards his whole body twitched, and he tossed his head with a snort of fright. But I kept a firm hold on the rope, and in a quiet voice as bold as I could make it I urged him forward.

He hesitated for only a moment, then took another step, and another. His body was like a coiled spring which I was afraid might break and flip us both over the rail. And there was little I could do. If he suddenly reared back, or shied, he would lose his footing, his weight would smash the railings, and we would be in the water. "Easy, fella," I whispered. "You can do it. Just one foot in front of the other. That's the way." Midway across the bridge I almost panicked and ran for it. "Attaboy! Easy. Easy."

Once Fiddler recognized that we were in danger—the increasing roar of the water must have alerted him in some \ ay—he seemed to grow utterly cool. His nervous trembling continued; his breathing didn't relax. But I sensed that he had placed himself in my hands. Step by step I led, and step by clicking step he followed.

But then as we neared the end of the bridge, the windbreaker began to slip out from where I had tucked it around the lariat halter. A corner of it flapped against Fiddler's face. He jerked his head high, and again the windbreaker slipped. It was loose enough now that Fiddler could glimpse the water tumbling beneath him. With a spasm of fear he lunged forward, breaking the handrail and knocking me to one side. As he passed I seized the improvised halter with one hand, and his mane with the other, and clung. The bridge was too narrow. Fiddler plunged over the side into the river, lunged powerfully, half turned, and lunged again. Clinging, I could feel his power clash with the force of the water.

I was under the surface, the current tearing at me. But as Fiddler plunged again and again, I clung, and when his hooves reached the bank and he heaved himself up, and almost fell back, and heaved again, my head came out into the air and I tried to fill my lungs. Once he had firm hold against the river bank, Fiddler leaped like a porpoise, each arc higher than the last, until he finally staggered out onto level ground. I would have expected him to pause and catch his breath, and say a prayer of thanksgiving, perhaps, and give me a chance to situate myself. I was there on sagging knees, my hands still clutching his rope and mane. But he didn't even hesitate—he just started ahead at a fast walk. With what felt like my last ounce of effort I bent my knees a little further and, launching myself upward, I caught my heel over Fiddler's back. "Whoa, boy." He wasn't listening. "Take it easy." Now he was trotting. Inch by inch I worked my body upward until my leg had good purchase on the other side of Fiddler's bouncing back. He broke into a gallop. Using what scrap of strength I had left in my arms, I pulled myself the rest of the way up, and there I lay, flat along his neck, as limp as drool. Faster he ran, and faster yet, the lariat flying behind us like a kite string. I caught it in my hand and began to

111

pull. At once the sound of his snorts increased, and he wildly tossed his head. I pulled the rope as hard as I could. I guess it cut off the wind where it crossed his nose. By pulling that lariat with all my strength, I was able at last to bring Fiddler to a lunging, turning, snorting, impatient stop. Then, fine-tuning the pressure on the lariat, I turned him and started at a walk toward the racetrack.

As I drew near I began to look for Sister Fender, or my folks, or someone who might tell me where she was. Surely by now she would have made her phone call. But nobody was paying any attention to what happened behind the grandstand. As I stretched my neck, I could see people clustered at the starting line, and horses and riders jogging up and down and then turning in under the wire. I tried to shout. I seemed to have neither voice nor breath. I tried again. Nothing.

A gunshot sounded; then a cheer. The race had started.

Twenty

I saw Marge Fender come running toward me, with the bridle in her hand. "It's too late," she said. "They've gone."

I pulled Fiddler to a stop. "What did the president say?"

Her frown disappeared. "Ryland's all right!" she cried. "He escaped!"

I felt as if I'd been struck by lightning; I couldn't even think. "Look out!" I cried.

"You've got to have a bridle . . ." she called after me.

But Fiddler was already running. And when people heard his hooves on the grass they turned and dived out of our way. At the edge of the track the spectators scattered like sheep, screaming. A couple of times I was afraid we were going to hit someome, but Fiddler broke stride just enough to brush by, and suddenly we were through them, with nothing in front of us but the empty track, and the field of horses just entering the first turn.

I laughed. It was crazy, of course, but I was full to the skin with elation. I had to do something wild. I felt the joyful surge of Fiddler's body under me. "Hah!" I cried, and leaned forward along his neck. I could feel the stretch and gather of his muscles as intimately as if they were part of me. With the lariat I tried to move him in close to the rail, but he resisted me. And then I noticed that the track on the far outside was almost dry; near the rail it was a sea of mud. I gave Fiddler his head.

I became aware that he was running with his nose slightly turned, as if to better counteract the tug of the lariat dragging behind us. Worse, it was picking up mud and getting heavier. I pulled myself further out onto his neck. With the very tips of my fingers I was able to reach the half hitch and push it over the end of his nose. Then I loosened the rope around his neck, and slid it over his ears and down until it dropped off and fell away. With a snort and a quick bob of his head, Fiddler seemed to dart forward. And I took both fists full of mane, and clung.

As we came into the backstretch the field was still ahead of us, though the distance had narrowed. In their scramble for position they had all moved in tight against the rail, their dark mass moving heavily through the mud. Not Fiddler. On the outside, he had found his place to run. Naked of saddle or bridle or any impediment except myself, he joyously tossed his head and charged. As we entered the clubhouse turn we drew even with the last horse. And coming into the stretch there were about four horses ahead of us, with Fetch Rhal on Queen of Spades leading by three lengths. His horse was running heavily, though, struggling against the mud, and weary with it. As we moved up on the right Fetch glanced back and saw us, and immediately forced Queen diagonally across the track in front of us.

"You have to look out for Fetch," Ry had warned me. "He doesn't carry that quirt to beat Queen with."

As soon as Queen hit the dry ground, she started to move. She was throwing mud like hailstones, but Fiddler didn't flinch. He moved his nose slowly up past her heels, past her flank, slowly past her shoulder. My body ached from clinging to him, and we were running so close together that I was afraid if Fiddler did pass her, Fetch's leg would brush me off.

"So you found him!" Fetch cried. "Well, it ain't goin' to do you any good."

I could see the finish line rushing toward us, and I could hear the cheering crowd, like distant thunder, but coming closer. I took a new fistful of mane in each hand and leaned as close to Fiddler's ear as I could get, and I shouted, "Hah! Go, fella, Hah!"

I caught a glimpse of Fetch Rhal's face, dark as a new moon and twisted with rage. Almost too fast to see, he flipped his wrist, and his quirt caught Fiddler smartly across the nose. It didn't work. Fiddler lunged furiously, and when Fetch saw that we were passing him, he shouted and ran his mare against us full force. At the same time he shoved the end of his quirt into my stomach as hard as he could. I almost blacked out, but I knew if Fiddler crossed the line without a rider his run would have been for nothing. I drew my knees up, and lying flat against his neck, I clung with every scrap of strength and consciousness I had. It wasn't enough. The pain continued to double me up, my mind turned to gauze and my fingers to noodles, and I started to slip away. I scarcely felt it when I hit the ground.

I was dimly aware of cheers and shouts and many people blocking out the light. Someone was washing my face, and holding ammonia under my nose. "You did it, Benny. You beat him." I realized it was my mother. I saw my dad smiling at me. I saw the bishop, looking a little water-soaked, but beaming. Teresa bent there, with tears streaming down her cheeks. And when I turned my head, I saw Sister Fender kneeling beside me.

"We won, Ben," she said. "You beat him, you and Fiddler. Wait till Ryland hears about this!"

One of the cowboys had roped Fiddler and brought

115

him back, and before I could ask Sister Fender about the telephone call they seized me and stood me beside her and Fiddler to have our pictures taken—first one of Fiddler with Sister Fender and me. And then another of her receiving the check. She endorsed it to Durwood Caswell, Sr., and handed it to him in front of everybody.

He stuttered and got all red, and fussed, and ended up giving it back to her. "This is for Ryland. Chalk it up to his missionary fund." Everybody cheered, and for the first time I saw Mr. Caswell take the hobbles off his smile. I thought his lips were going to pop from the unfamiliar exercise.

While we stood there smiling for the photographer, I whispered out of the side of my mouth. "Ry's free?"

Sister Fender whispered back, "I'm so excited I can hardly stand still."

"Hold it!" called the photographer.

"Where is he?"

"At the embassy in Bogota. He's flying to Washington tomorrow."

I couldn't talk. Joy and wonder filled my throat so full that for a minute it stopped my voice completely. Finally I blurted, "Thank heaven!"

"Yes," she said. "Nobody else could have done it."

She had a plane to catch. The president had invited her to be there with him when Ry and his companion arrived from Colombia. But as I walked with her to her car, Eli Rhal came across the grass and stopped us. He cussed like a mule skinner. "See, Marge?" he said. "I didn't have nothin' to do with kidnappin' your horse. Old Durwood Caswell done it, all the time."

He hadn't noticed that Durwood Caswell was right behind him, close enough to hear what he said. "Don't blame me for that."

"It was your barn," Eli said.

"I know," Durwood admitted. "And I guess it was my kid. Funny what a boy in love is capable of."

Sister Fender said, "He's no boy anymore, Durwood. I'm surprised you'd make excuses for him. Why on earth would he do it, anyway?"

"Tain't hard to figure," Eli said. "He knew if that Fiddler horse won, it would only set the little Lane filly to moonin' over Ry Fender again. Maybe he thought he was makin' progress, but I ain't seen no sign of it."

Durwood flushed. He was wearing a three-piece suit even today. I wondered if he had worn it while he bailed out his basement. "I don't mean to make excuses, Marge. I swear, as soon as I catch him I'll nail his hide to the barn door."

Sister Fender smiled sweetly. "Oh, you don't have to do that, Durwood. Just stringing him up by his thumbs will be all right."

"I'll do it," he vowed.

But we didn't wait around to see it happen. Nobody had seen Durwood Junior all day, anyway.

Twenty-One

For several days Sweet Willow was busy pumping out its cellars, dredging its ditches, and raking its yards. And about the time we might have sat back to draw breath and admire our clean little town, word came that Sister Fender was on her way home, and Ry and his companion were with her. Well, we didn't mind that sort of interruption. As they drove in from the airport and crossed the bridge at Banner about ten miles out, twenty-seven carloads of people were there to meet them.

When Teresa ran up to Ry, it was a picture. He stopped, and she stopped, and they stood there like a couple of reeds in a gale, being blown toward each other. "Bishop!" Ry cried at last. "What do I do now?"

Bishop West coughed unhappily. "Remember you're still a missionary."

"Can't you release me for just a minute?"

"I wasn't the one who called you. How can I release you?"

"Send a telegram to President Benson. Ask him . . ."

Somebody in the crowd cried, "Kiss her, for pete's sake."

That seemed to stop Ry. He backed away about half a step. "I love you, Terry. There's nothing wrong with me loving you."

"But you've been so far away," she said. "Can't you come a little closer than that?"

Ry said, "What does the handbook say, Bishop?"

"Not a word," the bishop replied. "You just have to use your judgment."

"Judgment?" Ry howled. "I don't have any judgment."

"Can you kiss her like you do your mother?" he asked.

"Are you kidding?" Ry glanced at his mother. "No offense, Mom."

"None taken," Sister Fender said. "I certainly wouldn't want you kissing me like you do her."

"Is a squeeze a sin?" Ry asked.

The bishop laughed. "Just no lip action."

With a cry Teresa flung herself into Ry's arms, and for a minute they stood hugging each other in front of the whole town. Her face was buried in his shoulder, and he bent, looking down at her. Then somebody started a car engine. We all scrambled into the cars and honked them ten miles back to town. There was a brief, formal greeting at the meetinghouse, since the day was too cool for the park, and then people went home to get ready for the banquet that night. I hadn't been able to get near Ry yet, but as he left the building I finally had a chance to tell him hello. When he saw me he hugged me like a long-lost brother; even invited me to lunch. When I got in the car I saw that Teresa had been invited too. Elder Jensen's parents had had to continue the plane journey to keep previous commitments, but would meet their son for his homecoming in a couple of days' time.

So there we were in the Fender kitchen, and while Sister Fender was busy at the stove, we boys and Teresa set the table and poured the milk. Ry's companion was a real cutup. We got started on a round of horseplay—popping the dishtowels at each other, and tossing biscuits back and forth, and Ry hanging a spoon from the end of his nose. He showed us how you have to breathe on the spoon first to make it stick. Elder Jensen tried it, and it worked, but I couldn't do it; I guess my nose was too skinny. We laughed till we were sick.

"Now you boys stop it," Sister Fender said. "You're undernourished, remember? You've got to take it easy."

"Shucks, Mom," Ry said. "We've been debriefed. We've had our medicals. All we need is one of your meals, and we'll be ready for anything."

"Well, at least wait until you eat it."

Watching Ry and Teresa together again, you could almost feel the attraction that sizzled between them, and yet they never touched. They seemed happy to honor Ry's missionary calling, and the standard of behavior that demanded of him. But surely there was nothing wrong with a little horseplay and clean fun; when you thought about what those elders had been through, our games seemed wholesome and restorative. Ry made a basketball out of a knotted dishtowel, and we played two-on, shooting at a bowl on the top cupboard. No matter how we raced across the floor and dodged back and forth, Ry and Teresa never touched. They were like two magnets that were pos-neg as they approached, and switched to pos-pos when they got too close. I kept waiting for Sister Fender to call a halt before we knocked her house down, but any time she wasn't busy at the stove she just sat in a chair well back from the action and watched us, smiling.

When the meal was ready, though, she said, "All right, that's enough." So we wound the game down, and started tussling to see who would sit in which chair. And when at last we were all primly seated and smiling, we saw that she was still standing behind her chair at the end of the table. "I don't know what today means to you," she said quietly.

121

She had been willing enough to let us have our fun, but now the time for games was over. "To me, it is like a resurrection, almost as if Ryland and Elder Jensen had returned from the dead."

The room had changed. Though echoes of our boisterousness lingered, the air was solemn now, even reverent. She continued. "I have offered my thanksgiving prayers, and since I heard that you boys were free, my heart has been full of gratitude every minute. But today, when we are here together for the first time, I would like to give our thanks again." We knelt beside our chairs. "Ryland," she said. "Would you call on someone to pray?"

He hesitated for a moment. "I think I'd like to do it myself."

It was not a long prayer. He didn't mention the gathering of Israel and the return of the lost tribes. What he talked about was the power of the gospel in our lives, and the need for us to carry its healing message to the world. He mentioned the bond of love that united the people in that room, and our joy in being together again. But most of all, he expressed his wonder at the love Jesus has for each one of us, and the way in which the Atonement gives us hope for eternal life. He closed by asking the Lord to help us live worthy of the things we had received.

After the prayer, it seemed nobody felt like talking. But there was too much that needed to be said for us to remain quiet very long. As we started to eat, the talk began, at first leading back to what had happened in Colombia. But then Ry said, "Tell us about the race, Ben."

"They took Fiddler hostage, too," I said.

"Yeah, I guess that was old Dur's idea?"

"I guess so." I didn't care about the race just then. I said, "How did you escape, Ry? What's it like to be a hostage?"

He looked at his companion. "What is it like, Elder?"

Elder Jensen shook his head. "It's not like anything. Not anything you ever did or knew about or imagined."

122

"The cold was the worst," Ry said. "No blankets—we had to sleep on the floor. That first night, we thought it would last forever. But as soon as morning came and we saw the filth we'd been sleeping in, we wished it was night again."

"The heat was the worst," Elder Jensen said.

"The bus ride was the worst," Ry corrected him.

Elder Jensen moaned. "Ohh! The bus ride. That bus must have been built in 1920, but I swear it was doing a hundred miles an hour. No headlights. Black as a tunnel. Roaring up that donkey trail, spitting gravel into the canyon every time we hit a curve. Passengers screaming. I knew I'd never see the sun again. O ye of little faith . . ."

"Actually, the house was the worst," Ry said. "Elder Jensen thought the food was the worst, because he said the house didn't crawl. But it did crawl—rats, bats, snakes, roaches; vines, slime, cobwebs. Ugh!"

"The guards were the worst," Elder Jensen said emphatically. "Rough? They looked like Attila's honor guard. Whiskers, bandoleras, guns, tequila—young, laughing, excited. 'Dos Americanos! Ahoo-ah!' "

"But their captain was a fat old dude," Ry said. "We called him Baby Fat—not to his face, mind you. He was forty, at least—sour. He just sneered at us and spit on the floor. He was the worst."

"Who were they?" I asked.

"Ordinary scum-bandits," Elder Jensen replied. "Ramon told us—you know Ramon? Our jailer? He told us they had taken hostages to bargain for the freedom of their leaders—to get them out of jail. But it turned out that all their leaders had been executed. Now we were no use to them. What would they do with us?"

Ry laughed. "Ah, Ramon. He was the littlest one of all—the youngest, the most fanatical. Baby Fat told us that he had chosen Ramon to guard us because if we tried to get away, he knew that Ramon would not hesitate to shoot us. 'Yan-kee!' Ramon would say. 'Yan-kee! What you doing here? You come down here to get yourself dead. You come to right place. Yan-kee!'

"He spoke English pretty well—turned out he'd lived with relatives in Los Angeles for a while. Still, he swore better in Spanish. And since he spoke so fast I couldn't understand him, Elder Jensen would translate and bippie over the cuss words. It'd drive Ramon wild."

"But he got his revenge," Elder Jensen said. "Sometimes when he was mad at us, he'd bring our supper in and feed it to the rats. He'd put the plates against the wall, and then sit there smiling, with his gun in his hands, and watch the rats eat our food."

Ry added, "The awful thing was that we were so hungry we really wanted to eat the stuff. If he'd let us, we'd have fought the rats for it."

Sister Fender shuddered. "How did you ever stand it?"

"We really didn't have much choice," Ry said.

"But you did escape," I said.

"It's a matter of incentive," Elder Jensen said. "We thought we had tried everything. But you see, when you want to do something badly enough . . ." His voice dropped, and switched into a phony backwoods dialect. "Y'see, in this particular town the roadhouse, it was on one side, and the town, it was on the other, and the cemetery, it was in between. And late one dark night this little old drunk tries to find his way home." Elder Jensen stood up and began to cross the kitchen, demonstrating how the drunk walked, shuffling this way and that. "It's so late, man, he knows his wife is goin' to skin him when he gets home, so he tries to hurry up. He decides to cut across the graveyard, and, Boom! What do you think? He falls into an open grave. But he's cool, man. He don't get excited. He knows that's bad for the heart. He stands up and tries to crawl out of the grave. 'Course, there's no way—straight walls six feet high and slick as mud, nothing to grab onto. He jumps and shouts and scrambles for an hour. He plumb wears himself out. But he sees it's no good. He'll just have to stay in that grave all night. He sees that. And he sinks down in the corner of that grave—man, he's shakin' all over, he's so scared.

"But tain't long comes another little drunk waltzin' through the graveyard and, Oops! He falls into that same grave, too. Man, how he jumps and scratches and yells, but it don't do no good. Straight walls, six feet high, slick as mud, nothin' to grab onto. He plumb wears himself out. And finally he just sinks down there in that dark, cold old grave, puffin', and shiverin', he's so scared."

Elder Jensen's tone changed again—he spoke in his normal voice, every word clear and precise. "So the first drunk felt sorry for the little dude, and he leaned over and tapped him on the shoulder, and said, 'Man, you can't get out of here.'

"But he did."

I laughed, and Sister Fender laughed, and Teresa laughed, while Ry explained. "We couldn't escape from that horrible old castle, either."

And Elder Jensen, laughing at his own joke, said, "But we did."

"You see, they had decided to kill us," Ry said. And we all laughed like clowns, as if killing them was the funniest thing since a feathered grizzly.

But when we had settled down a little, Sister Fender said, "It's not very funny, is it?"

"It sure wasn't funny then," Ry said.

And Elder Jensen said, "I couldn't understand it. To me, it seemed that all they had to do was turn us loose. But I guess Baby Fat was afraid we'd give away his hiding place. We couldn't if we wanted to—we didn't even know which side of the equator we were on."

Ry went on. "But Ramon told us that the captain had made up his mind. He had no choice; he would have to kill us."

"So we had the incentive," said Elder Jensen, "but we had no heart for it. We were discouraged. We'd prayed for so long, and nobody seemed to be listening. I know it seems weak, but we were weak. Even if they didn't kill us, we didn't see how we could live much longer. We felt alone, almost forgotten."

"I hadn't forgotten you," Teresa said.

And Ry added, "The Lord hadn't forgotten us, either."

Sister Fender said, "How could he, with so many people reminding him every day?"

Ry shook his head. "It seems strange now to realize how low in spirit we had become. But when you are there, and months pass when you're completely shut off, it's hard to realize how many people are concerned about you, and praying for you. And I have to tell you that Elder Jensen was kidding you just now. Weak? Not him. There may have been moments when he got a little concerned, but weak? He doesn't know what weak is. Let me tell you what he did.

"He said he knew that Ramon was right—that all we needed was the faith of Alma, and the Lord would deliver us. So the night before we were to be executed, he had the three of us (Ramon was there, you understand) kneel in that horrible, dark, crawling room. And he prayed aloud. And then I prayed. And then Ramon prayed. And with every prayer the darkness withdrew a little more. I don't mean that we could see any better; I mean that we felt bathed in a miraculous radiance that seemed to fill our beings with light, enabling our eyes, that could not make out the wall of the room, to somehow pierce the mysteries of heaven."

There was a long silence; not a dead silence, but one alive with the wonder of what had happened, and this chance we had to share in it, however distantly.

Ry continued. "When I raised my head, I could see the

whites of Ramon's eyes. 'I go,' he said, and raised from his knees. 'The walls will not hurt you.'

"Elder Jensen took his arm. 'The walls won't fall on you either, will they?'

"Ramon's eyes seemed to grow bigger. It was almost as if the light in his eyes intensified with the increasing fire of his faith. 'No,' he said.

" 'How do you know?' Elder Jensen asked him.

"Ramon hesitated, staring at Elder Jensen with those huge white eyes. At last he said, 'You don't need an earthquake.' It seemed hard for him to finish what he had to say. But he did it, in a voice vibrant with conviction. 'You got me.'

" 'Yes,' he said. 'You are our earthquake, Ramon.'

"I realized that I had known it, too. While we were praying, I had come to understand that Ramon would save us. We all had."

" 'Do you know what you're going to do?' Elder Jensen asked.

"Again, Ramon hesitated. 'I will be back,' he said, and left the room.

"We waited, for hours, it seemed. But we had no way to tell. They had taken our watches away from us on the first night. Time had become meaningless. One night, while we were lying there on the floor waiting for morning, Elder Jensen told me a story about what happened at Owl Creek Bridge. They hanged a young man from the bridge, but just at the last minute he escaped and ran away, trying to make it back to the arms of his sweetheart. The story goes into great detail about his escape. And just when at last he had reached safety, he also reached the end of his rope, literally. His whole escape had been nothing more than a fantasy created by his mind as he dropped from the bridge—hours of action compressed into a split second of time. Of course, the story is preposterous—how could

127

anyone know what flashed through the young man's mind in the final moment of his life? But the point is, I suppose, that we humans have no pendulum in our head, and the length of our minutes and days is as fickle as the wind, ruled more by our emotions than by the motion of the planets.''

"Okay, okay," Elder Jensen said. "Enough already. Tell the story."

Ry looked at him with wide, innocent eyes. "Look who's talking. You can dish it out, but you can't take it."

"I never got sidetracked that bad."

"You should have heard him," Ry said. "Day after day in that rats' nest he would lecture me on the joys of misery—quoting Shakespeare, for pete's sake. 'Sweet are the uses of adversity,' or something."

Elder Jensen continued:

Which, like the toad, ugly and venomous,
Wears yet a precious jewel in his head;
And this our life, exempt from public haunt,
Finds tongues in trees, books in the running brooks,
Sermons in stones, and good in every thing:
I would not change it.

"You tell the story," Ry said.

His companion coughed. "Well, I couldn't sleep a wink. Figure it for yourself. In the morning they were going to kill us—hardly the kind of thing to make you drowsy. But Elder Fender was fast asleep, his breath as sweet as a tuba. That was the hardest part of all."

"Not me," Ry corrected him. "I didn't close my eyes all night."

"Listen." Elder Jensen looked at Sister Fender, and then at Teresa, and then at me. "I'll tell you what happened. Sometime during the night we heard the door open. Very quietly, mind you, but we heard it. Footsteps crossing the floor. I wondered if they were coming to cut our throats

128

and save the bullets. But then a voice whispered, 'Are you awake?' It was Ramon. 'Follow me,' he said.

"We followed him, silently creeping out of the door, down the stairs, across the hall, into the patio. In the shadow of the gate he hissed, 'Wait here.' And even in the darkness I could see that Ramon had changed. No longer brash and over-aggressive, he had become measured and confident—he had become the comandante. He hurried across the yard and disappeared into the darkness of the jungle. Scarcely a moment passed before we heard the roar of an engine. An old truck came rocketing out of the shadows and stopped beside us. Ramon was at the wheel. 'Vengate!' he cried. 'Come!' And even as we scrambled aboard he drove off down the road, switching on his headlights as he rounded the first bend.

"I thought, 'Ramon has gone crazy. We will never escape. The captain will chase us in his jeep, and machine-gun us.' But Ramon was laughing. 'Ahoo-ah!' he cried. Driving furiously down the road with one hand, he reached down and raised in the other what looked, in the darkness, like a fistful of dead worms—the distributor caps from all the other vehicles at the camp. 'We got a tankful of gas!' he cried. 'Where you want to go?' "

Ry said, "We went straight to the mission home. And when we had eaten and bathed and eaten and rested and eaten, the first thing we did was baptize Ramon."

Elder Jensen nodded. "You should have seen his face shine when he came out of the water. And I thought, *This is how Alma must have looked.*"

Ry said, "We told him we were going to take him hostage and bring him with us back to the United States."

"Do you know what he said?" Elder Jensen asked. " 'You're too late,' he said. 'I'm already a hostage of the Lord. I will become a missionary among my own people, and instead of killing them I will save them.' "

"Hey, Ry," I said. "I get all mixed up. What is a hostage, anyway?"

"A hostage is a prisoner."

"Not just any garden-type prisoner, though."

"No. A temporary prisoner, held captive until someone else keeps his promise. Like Damon and Pythias."

"The guy who was going to be hanged if his friend didn't get back in time?"

"That's the one."

"But Ramon called himself a hostage of the Lord."

"Well," Ry said. "Paul talked about being a prisoner of Jesus Christ."

"That's not the same."

"No, it isn't," Ry agreed. He seemed to ponder. "I guess a prisoner of God is one so committed to the Lord that he can never escape his covenants. You know, like a man who couldn't lie would be a prisoner of truth."

"And a hostage?" I asked.

Ry hesitated.

Elder Jensen suggested, "You have to be careful how you relate the two, I think. This is the way it seems to me: A hostage is a prisoner who is waiting to be ransomed. In that sense we are all hostages. But Christ kept his promise—he was a ransom for all. And when you and I accept that, we become free."

Nobody spoke. We all seemed to be sorting out what had been said. Finally, Teresa asked, "Are you going back to Colombia?"

"We don't know," Ry said. "We'll finish our missions, but they haven't told us where yet."

"I don't think I could stand it," she said.

"Don't say that," Ry told her. "You could stand it. I have to admit I'd like to go back."

"You must be joking," she said.

"No. I really would. Wouldn't you, Elder?"

Elder Jensen nodded his head. "There are so many good people there. And besides, it would be wonderful to watch Ramon preach the gospel."

Teresa's eyes were teary, but she smiled. "All right, I can stand it. But no more being taken hostage."

Elder Jensen laughed. "We're dedicated missionaries," he said. "You know, whatever it takes. If that's the only way we can find someone to baptize." In a minute or so he had Teresa laughing, too.

At last Ry leaned over, and put his arm across my shoulder. "Now, you tell us *your* story."

My story? I couldn't imagine what he was talking about. My mind was so full of Ry and his companion, and Ramon, that right then it seemed there was nothing else in the world.

Ry turned to Elder Jensen. "This is the kid I was telling you about—the greatest jockey in the world."

"Not as good as you, Ry," I said.

"The new Willie Shoemaker."

"Cut it out," I said.

"And that isn't all. He's going to make the greatest missionary."

What a joker! I told him, "Not as good as you."

"The new LeGrand Richards." Ry looked at me. "You think I'm kidding, don't you? But you've already proved you're a winner, Ben. You can be anything you want."

He was serious. I thought maybe it wouldn't hurt me to be serious for once, myself. "I want to be like Ramon," I said. "I want to be a hostage—a prisoner of God."